Praise for

Courting Miss *Cartwright*

I0531436

"I loved all of the stories in this collection--they were well-written and I liked the characters, My favorite, though, has to be Kristin Holt's "Courting Miss Cartwright." Not only was Rocky a "mensch" (a good guy), I was pleasantly surprised to see that he used Yiddish expressions that me, my parents and grandparents used and they were woven into the story. I liked Felicity and Temperence (after I got to know her) as well. Rocky's surrogate Jewish parents, Mikkail and Ana, were great--I hope they get a story."
~ 5 stars, Reviewer: Nancy Levine "Nancy"

"A touching story about Felicity and her half-sister Temperance. Rocky is torn between courting one sister and falling in love with another. What will his choice be? And will that choice tear apart the bond that the sisters have just found with each other? An emotional tale of what a child out of wedlock faced in days gone by."

~ 5 stars, Reviewer: C. Patterson

"I liked how this story is not your typical story. To spin a story where two people are against each other and come together for the best of the family is not always the easiest thing however K. Holt pulled it off splendidly. I couldn't wait to finish the book to find out what happened with the two sisters."

~ 5 stars: Cowgirl2Fireman

Note: This novella was previously published within the Western Historical Romance Multi-author Boxed Set *Cowboys & Calico*. These reviews specifically referenced Courting Miss Cartwright within that boxed set.

"*D*id I ask for kindness?"

"No, and you didn't need to. You're a lady, and you deserve every modicum of respect."

With sudden awareness, he realized this firecracker of a woman stood so near, essentially in the circle of his arms. She'd tipped her face up to his, the better to yell at him. So near, the fragrance of her freshly washed hair teased his senses.

He thumbed a bit of *shmutz* from her cheek.

Her nostrils flared. Her eyes rounded.

And just like that, he knew she was every bit as affected. *Irresistible*. One little dip of his head, a *bissel* closer…

Their mouths pressed, motionless… Held.

Without conscious intent, the intimate touch became a kiss. Powerful. Demanding and hungry.

His heart nearly seized as she participated, wholly, kissing *him*.

The fist to his gut nearly knocked him on *his tuches*. Sanity screamed at him to halt, to control himself. But it felt so darn good—so right, so—

She wrenched free, her chest heaving, her wild expression made him want another kiss. No, a *hundred* more.

But…he'd kissed Felicity as if he'd never wanted anyone more.

When he'd all but promised to wed Temperance.

He soundly berated himself. The horror of his impetuous actions chased away the lingering glow. Dozens of sermons by the departed minister swamped his consciousness, reminding him of his duties, his obligations, how a gentleman *must* control his passions. The preacher had known all about the dangers inherent in giving in to desire.

How had he lost himself in the craziness?

He'd just kissed *his future sister-in-law*.

Dedication

*W*ith fond appreciation to Rocky Palmer: friend, supporter, avid reader, and copy editor. Your love of western historical romance is exceeded only by your capacity to find and eradicate errors large and small. You're my (literary) hero. Thank you for loaning me your name. It was a pleasure naming a hero after you.

Courting Miss *Cartwright*

Mountain Home, Colorado
July, 1879

Courtship, by the book, is supposed to be easy...

As the daughter of an unwed mother, <u>Felicity Percival</u> is accustomed to rejection. Her mother was her only family...until she is summoned to the reading of her father's will. To learn he was a married preacher with a second daughter horrifies her. Having a half-sister she doesn't want appalls her. The stipulations attached to her inheritance infuriate her. The last thing she expects is the emergence of truths that destroy her life-long beliefs. The last thing she wants is to feel the blush of first love for a man she can't have.

The road to Happily Ever After should not be rocky, especially for level-headed, rule-following <u>Rocky</u>

<u>Gideon</u>. His courtship of the minister's legitimate daughter is successful and on track, surviving everything life throws at them...except the appearance of the preacher's *other* daughter. Felicity asks too many questions, reminds him of his distant past, fights off a pack of petticoated she-wolves, forces him to evaluate his carefully constructed plan, and somehow steals his heart.

Rocky desperately needs a stable, solid marriage that will go the distance...so why does he yearn for the wrong sister?

Courting Miss Cartwright

Courting Miss *Cartwright*

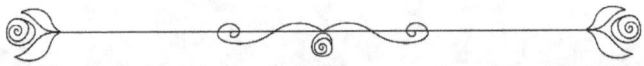

A Sweet Western Historical Romance Novella (Rated PG)

Six Brides for Six Gideons Series, Book #2
and
A Holidays in Mountain Home Novella

By
KRISTIN HOLT

The books in this series are loosely connected and may be read in any order.
*Note: Books 1 and 2 are entirely unrelated as the lost brothers have not yet reconnected.

Chapter One

"Courtship's sole purpose is to bring about your marriage to a well-suited woman. Courtship, executed properly, will develop a lasting bond certain to surmount life's difficulties."
~ *The Gentleman's Guide to Courtship and Marriage*

Mountain Home, Colorado
Monday, July 7, 1879

ROCKY GIDEON'S rotten mood darkened tenfold.

The reading of Cedric Cartwright's last will and testament was supposed to be simple. Quick. Just immediate family.

And no surprises.

Never had he suspected the family attorney, W.W. Stuart, would enter his office with a most unwelcome bit of history trailing behind.

That bit of unwelcome history had a name: *Felicity Percival*.

Rocky had never met the young woman, but her identity was unmistakable, given she looked more like Cartwright than Cartwright himself.

The news would undoubtedly invoke a grand pyrotechnic display.

He doubted Temperance knew about Felicity...hence the impending fireworks.

Temperance reclined on the settee and fanned herself. Her eyes closed, her crossed ankles in shiny button-up shoes rested on the upholstery.

Mr. Stuart hung his hat on the coat tree and dropped his leather satchel beside it. Without a word, he took his seat behind his heavy oak desk. "Let's begin." He withdrew a folder from a drawer and opened it.

Stuart's youth showed in a head of thick blond hair and a hint of fullness about his cheeks. The boy looked too young to practice law. But his credentials had checked out and The Reverend Cartwright had trusted him.

Temperance shifted, glancing at Stuart, then took notice of Felicity Percival, halted awkwardly in the middle of the room. "Mr. Stuart? Who is this?"

Rocky braced his arms on the back of Temperance's settee and watched his sweetheart. *If* she knew about Felicity Percival, she'd put two and two together.

"Miss Cartwright." W.W. Stuart nodded at Temperance with deference. "Mr. Rocky Gideon, may I introduce Miss Felicity Percival, of St. Louis."

Still no recognition. *Not good.*

"Miss Percival, Miss Cartwright is the sole surviving child of The Reverend and Mrs. Cedric Cartwright, both of whom are recently deceased."

Ah, so carefully worded.

Miss Percival gave a jerking nod, then set down a satchel as dusty and careworn as her person. As if stupefied by the news of another offspring, she clasped one hand over her mouth, the other tightly about her waist. Perhaps she'd burst into laughter, tears, or hysterics. She lowered herself with excruciating slowness into a hard-seated chair.

"I don't understand." Temperance folded her fan with a snap. Her boots landed on the carpet with a muffled thud. "I know all my cousins. Who are you, Miss Percival?"

Rocky clenched his fists, squeezed his eyes shut, and cursed Cedric Cartwright soundly in Yiddish *and* English. Shame on Cedric for divulging his past to his sweet, tender-hearted daughter in this manner. Shame on him for doing this to *both* daughters.

Felicity straightened her spine. She eyed Temperance, then Rocky, ultimately turning her attention squarely on the attorney. "Mr. Stuart, I believe the responsibility for a thorough introduction falls to you, sir."

Rocky had to respect the woman's mettle.

"I comprehend Miss Cartwright. Why don't you begin," Miss Percival continued, her gaze never leaving Stuart, "by explaining who Mr. Gideon is?"

With a sigh, Stuart stood and circled the desk. "Mr. Gideon is courting Miss Cartwright. He is here, no doubt, to safeguard her interests, though I assure you her father did."

Rocky pressed a comforting hand on Temperance's shoulder. Fireworks in five, four, three...

"Miss Percival," Stuart gestured with a flourish, "is named in the will as she is also a direct descendant of Ced—"

"*What?*" Temperance shrieked. She shrugged Rocky's touch away. Bright pink splotched her pale cheeks.

"Miss Percival," Stuart repeated, "is also your father's daughter."

"*No, no, no.*" Temperance wilted.

Rocky reached for her even as she collapsed in a faint.

With his jaw locked, he gently laid Temperance back on the settee. He slipped around the couch and lifted her feet onto the upholstery. He opened her lace and silk fan and waved it before her face, trying to give her some air. "What were you thinking, man, to deliver word like that without preparing her? Make yourself useful and fetch smelling salts."

"I'LL PROCEED with the reading of the will." Stuart turned in his chair to catch the slanted rays of sunlight streaming through the west-facing windows.

Rocky braced his arms on the back of the settee, acutely aware of both women.

Recovered from her swoon and silently weeping into her hankie, Temperance reclined on the settee before him. Felicity Percival, the illegitimate daughter, sat with her spine rigid in the hard chair to his left. This wasn't an easy situation for either sister.

Stuart stood and paced to the window, putting the daylight at his back. "The Reverend Cedric Adams Cartwright, late of Church Street, Mountain Home, Colorado, died on the 2nd of July, 1879, having duly made his last will and testament on Tuesday, the 18th of March, 1879, in words and figures following:—

"I, Cedric A. Cartwright, widower, hereby revoke all wills and other testamentary dispositions heretofore made by me, and declare this to be my last will and testament. I give and bequeath unto Miss Temperance Annelise Cartwright the entirety of her mother's inheritance, five hundred, seventy-six dollars and ninety-three cents, currently in the bank at Mountain Home, to be received by her one year from the date of the reading of this will, upon the suitable completion of my stipulations."

Rocky pushed upright. "What stipulations?"

Stuart gestured for silence but didn't bother to look up. "I give and bequeath unto Miss Felicity Percival the entirety of a bank account at the aforementioned banking establishment, in her name, containing the sum of five hundred, seventy-six dollars and ninety-three cents, to be released one year from the date of the reading of this will, upon the suitable completion of my stipulations."

A fortune, especially to a woman dressed so poorly, in *shamatta*. Rags.

"In the intervening year, which shall commence on the date my last will and testament is read to Miss Felicity Percival and to Miss Temperance Cartwright, my two daughters—"

Temperance's groan put Rocky in mind of a mewling kitten. Thank God she'd remained lying down.

The attorney flinched as if realizing the pain and suffering he'd caused.

Rocky put a calming hand on his sweetheart's shoulder.

"—my stipulations to them, governing the receipt of their inheritances, shall be as follows:

"Miss Felicity Percival shall be known both publicly and privately as Miss Felicity Cartwright."

Temperance whimpered.

Rocky risked a glance at the illegitimate daughter, set to inherit nearly *five hundred and seventy-seven dollars*, the family name, and who knew what else. The girl seemed as upset—if not more—than Temperance.

Why?

"My daughters Felicity and Temperance—"

Cartwright listed his illegitimate daughter *before* Temperance?

"—shall be joint inhabitants of the Cartwright home, adjacent to the church lot. They shall live together with the purpose of coming to know one another as sisters."

Felicity shook her head in vehement denial.

The attorney ignored her, as did Temperance. Rocky decided following suit was the safest course of action and ignored her too.

"Upon Temperance's soon-to-occur marriage to Mr. Rocky Gideon, the Cartwright house shall become the full and legal property of my daughter, Felicity Cartwright—"

The minister had visited the fashionable and large two-story residence Rocky had begun building for his bride. He'd known Temperance would be well cared for, the wife of one of the wealthiest men in the county. She wouldn't need the Cartwright home, but she'd want it. Rocky's heart twisted.

"—providing," continued the attorney with strong emphasis on that codicil, "she remains in Mountain Home for a minimum of one year. If not, the money shall be forfeit and transferred to the church's directors. The house shall be likewise given to the church, upon Temperance's marriage."

Felicity again shook her head in silent refusal.

If not an inheritance, what did she want?

"To provide for the support of my daughters, the household account is available to my daughter Temperance, whom I trust to ensure the day to day needs of her sister are met."

Temperance sniffled and blew her nose into her lace-trimmed hankie.

"The bank accounts in reserve for each daughter shall be released to them in one year's time if, by the estimation of my executor, William Woodward Stuart, Attorney at Law, Miss Temperance and Miss Felicity have treated one another with *fairness*," Stuart emphasized, "*kindness*," he paused, "and *equity*."

Perplexed, mystified, Rocky sucked in a deep breath. "How, precisely, do you imagine to quantify kindness or equity, Mr. Stuart? A man might gauge ore cut from a mine or determine ounces of silver. But *fairness*? How do you suppose you'll measure fairness?"

"I assure you," the lawyer said, his voice calm, "I'm quite capable of evaluating such matters."

What on earth had Cartwright been thinking to entrust Stuart with this loosey-goosey judgment call?

This whole thing stank! Rocky locked his jaw, determined to hear the rest of the blasted will, *then* put a stop to the fiasco.

He had enough money, enough persuasion in this town to hire his own lawyer, one who'd certainly have Temperance's best interests at heart. He'd fight the will, see to it she received everything she had coming without trying to measure up to absurd postmortem demands.

Maybe he'd just walk away, take Temperance with him. He had more than enough to provide for his wife, *far* more than her father.

But one glance between the two women, eying one another warily, and he realized the money, the property, even the Cartwright name wasn't the problem.

Oh, no.

Blast Cedric Cartwright's selfish hide.

Beyond the grave, without an ounce of explanation of how this whole mess came to be, expected—no, *demanded*—his daughters accept one another as sisters.

As far as he could see? Not going to happen.

Chapter Two

"Consistently treat ladies of all ages and rank with
great respect and deference."
~ *The Gentleman's Guide to Courtship and Marriage*

FELICITY'S HEART slammed against her ribs, a hot,
hard fist that stole her wind.

Her father—*a preacher*!

Who was The Reverend Cartwright that he
dared demand she live in Mountain Home?

She didn't want her father's money.

She didn't want his house.

She did *not* want this previously unknown half-
sister. Well-dressed in pastel yellow, embroidered

summer cotton, bustled and curled and expensive, the woman's pale skin had never seen a day's work. Miss Temperance's expression registered abhorrence and disdain when the attorney had introduced Cedric's *other* daughter.

Felicity wanted nothing from either of them.

Questions churned but one fought for dominance—the horrid probability that blonde, blue-eyed Temperance was older than she, and Mother's liaison with Cedric Cartwright had occurred during his marriage. "What is your age?"

Miss Cartwright gasped with outrage. "How old are *you*?"

Maybe the preacher's daughter possessed a bit of spunk.

"Ladies, ladies." Stuart dropped the document on his desktop. "No need for hysterics."

He rounded the desk, his bearing commanding attention. "Miss Felicity is twenty-five years of age, Miss Temperance. She was born a few months after your parents' marriage."

Thank God.

"Miss Temperance," he continued, addressing Felicity, "was born September 7, 1858. She will soon be twenty-one."

"When was he ordained?" Felicity addressed the lawyer. She doubted Temperance would forfeit information.

"I don't rightly know. Temperance?"

Felicity's blood had reached a boil. She didn't wait for a reply. "I want to know. Was he—" *the sanctimonious, self-serving—* "a minister of the gospel when he seduced my mother?"

"Miss Percival," Stuart ordered, "mind your tongue."

"Answer my question." Fisting her skirts in her hands, her jaw locked, she forced her gaze to remain steady on the attorney. "*Please.*"

"I don't believe your question justifies an answer."

All her life people treated her with contempt, merely for her lack of married parents. Given Cartwright had caused this blight upon her life, she deserved answers. She'd opened her mouth to say so, but Mr. Gideon spoke first.

"I recall hearing he was ordained shortly after his marriage to Mrs. Cartwright." He flicked a glance toward Felicity, then back to Miss Temperance. "Isn't that right, sweetheart?"

Just as she was well acquainted with verbal rudeness, she'd experienced plenty of folks unwilling to meet her eye. It seemed Temperance, also, had acquired an allergy to persons born on the wrong side of the blanket. The young woman answered Mr. Gideon's question in the affirmative and met his gaze. He, apparently, had the privilege of birth on the *correct* side of the proverbial blanket.

Felicity didn't know whether to feel relieved or exhausted. Or both.

"Now that wasn't so hard," Mr. Rocky Gideon said, the set of his jaw and the spark in his brown eyes drilling holes in the attorney, "now was it, Mr.

Stuart?"

The lawyer muttered something unintelligible. He, too, looked anywhere but at her.

No skin off her nose. She didn't need or want anything further from Cartwright's man.

She glanced away from the attorney and met Mr. Gideon's gaze quite by mistake.

Something flickered in his eyes, brief, but powerful. He *knew* something! About the timing of Cartwright's ordination? About Felicity's mother?

Mr. Gideon couldn't yet be into his thirties. Not a contemporary of Cartwright's, so whatever he knew, or thought he knew, wasn't gained by personal observation.

He glanced away, breaking eye contact.

Oh, he definitely *knew* something.

Desperation made her bold—she'd ask him, outright, but sensed the man had good reason for remaining silent. Loyalty to Miss Cartwright, certainly, and a desire to safeguard the minister's reputation from further damage.

The interview had outlived its usefulness.

Shaking with anger, awash with questions that wouldn't subside, she pushed to her feet and when the attorney finally deigned to look at her, she met his gaze squarely. Seconds ticked past, marked by the clock on the mantle. "Mr. Stuart, I must respectfully decline the terms of Mr. Cartwright's last will and testament. I want nothing from the man who cavalierly dismissed my mother and me."

She picked up her carpetbag, clenching her fist

around the handle, then forced herself to meet her half-sister's eyes. "I won't be troubling you, Miss Cartwright. Good evening."

Goodbye and good riddance.

"I'M PROUD of you," Rocky told Temperance as he escorted her through the attorney's front door. "Your father would be proud too." She'd skated close to the edge a time or two, but given the unwelcome news, she'd done better than anyone could expect.

"Thank you, Rocky." Her voice sounded small, fragile, as if the light had fled her soul. She accepted the arm he offered but the spring was gone from her step. "I wasn't prepared for..." she waved her gloved hand as if to indicate the unwelcome news. "What am I to do?"

Outside, the air proved at least ten degrees cooler than in the office. He drew a deep lungful and tipped her beautiful face up. "We'll figure it all out. Together."

A little nod, a weak smile. Seeing her like this broke his heart.

Cartwright *owed* his daughter better. He clamped his jaw rather than say so.

One thing was certain, he'd never withhold important information from his sweetheart. She could count on him.

Temperance looked up. "Thank you for attending the reading with me."

"I'm honored to be at your side, no matter what comes." He covered her hand upon his arm with his own. "I believe the worst is behind us."

Strolling at his side, she sighed. Exhaustion mingled with grief in that single huff. "I hope so."

Mrs. Pettingill and Mrs. Whipple conversed on the boardwalk between their establishments, the tailor shop and bakery. Both women swept dust into the street.

"Evening, Mr. Gideon, Miss Cartwright." Mrs. Pettingill leaned her broom against her shop and, with a quick glance both directions on the street, crossed the dirt track toward them. Mrs. Whipple followed. "How are you getting along, my dear?"

Temperance smiled and took their hands in her own, assured them she was well. Engaged by the women, she didn't notice Miss Felicity Percival exit the train depot at her back.

But Rocky took note.

He saw.

Boy, did he.

Desperation darkened Felicity Percival's eyes and rounded her narrow shoulders.

In that briefest of moments, the gist of the woman's plight crystallized.

With no train coming through until tomorrow, she was stuck in Mountain Home overnight. But her simple calico, old shoes, and mostly empty carpetbag made him suspect Temperance's half-sister couldn't pay for a night's lodging and meals, much less passage back to St. Louis.

Miss Percival was in a fix.

Nothing made him as antsy as a woman in need.

If he didn't help, where would she turn?

To W.W. Stuart? The man who'd brought her to town for the reading of the will, scolded her, and let her walk out of his office without escort and nowhere to go? The *shmendrik*. Useless excuse for a man.

Miss Percival blinked and that spare second passed.

Temperance must have heard the footfalls sounding on the boardwalk for she turned, and finding the source of her recent distress, nodded in acknowledgment. Ever the proper Christian lady.

What had Felicity said in the agitated exchange, not ten minutes earlier? Her certainty that Cedric Cartwright had seduced her mother?

That told quite a tale. People could be downright mean to women who bore children alone, even in the West. Folks like that tended to let their pious venom seep onto innocent children.

He may have been born to married parents but he knew, far too well, what self-righteous attitudes cost a child. In Miss Percival, he witnessed another like himself. An outcast, an invisible, one who'd suffered much. She'd learned to cope with the rotten hand dealt her.

A curt nod in his direction, and she strode with

purpose down the walk, probably to Ihnken's boardinghouse. He wouldn't be surprised to learn she'd asked after lodgings upon discovering herself stranded in Mountain Home.

"Wait." Rocky took an unconscious step after Miss Felicity—only to come to himself, Temperance's gloved hand tucked into the crook of his arm.

Felicity halted, turned back.

He removed a dollar from his pocketbook and extended it to her. "For lodging and a meal." He glimpsed her intention to refuse. "Take it."

He felt Temperance's gaze on him, silently full of questions.

Felicity lifted her chin. "I don't need your money, Mr. Gideon."

Maybe she'd brought a little *gelt*—money—with her. Maybe Stuart had given her funds to cover a night's lodging and meals until she returned home.

Maybe he hadn't.

He waited, the dollar so much more than a peace offering. He *needed* to ensure this woman's comfort.

"No, thank you. I can take care of myself." With a brisk shake of her head, Felicity departed.

Rocky owed his allegiance to Temperance. So why the desperation to see to Miss Percival?

With a force of will, he ignored his conscience, stuffed his dollar back in his pocketbook, and gave his sweetheart his full attention.

"Thank you." Temperance smiled at the older women. "You're both so thoughtful."

"Goodnight, Mrs. Pettingill," he added, "Mrs. Whipple. It's good to see you both."

Temperance seemed content to stroll in silence at his side without conversation.

They waved at friends, spoke briefly to neighbors, and by the time they'd rounded the corner and the church came into view, the Cartwright home on the adjacent lot, he knew what he had to do.

Tomorrow, he'd pay Miss Percival a call, make sure she had the funds necessary to see herself home on the train.

It was the least he could do.

Chapter Three

"Whenever possible, see you do not disappoint your intended. Ensure you are at her side when she needs you most."
~ *The Gentleman's Guide to Courtship and Marriage*

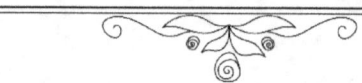

TEMPERANCE wanted nothing more than to go home and shut herself away from the public eye.

Hot tears threatened and her throat filled. Betrayal, sharp and insistent, clawed at her resolve.

At last they reached home. Rocky opened the back door and ushered her inside.

She drew a deep breath, savoring the fragrance of Mother's yellow roses blooming beside the stoop.

She wanted Rocky to go, to leave her alone to peel off the layers of clothing and bathe. She wanted to retire and rest. Or maybe she wanted him to stay.

"Sit down, sweetheart. I'll start tea." He worked the pump and filled the kettle. "Are you hungry?"

"Just tea, thank you." She untied her bonnet ribbons.

He fueled the stove, set the kettle on, and watched her with gentle kindness. Concern etched his features in the fading daylight. "Are you well?"

"Very well, thank you." It wouldn't do to let him see her so shaken. After all, everyone complimented how well she'd held up.

"You suffered a shock." He sat beside her, the warmth of his presence her anchor in the storm. Always, her anchor.

"Indeed." Again, unwelcome tears threatened. "I pray Mother never knew."

"I doubt he told her. His example proved him better than that."

"He was a good and loving husband." And father. "Why did he bring *her* here?"

"I expect it's just as the will states. He wanted you to have a chance to know your—" He winced. "Sorry."

Sister.

The thought, so repugnant, so...*shameful.*

With elbows propped on the tabletop, she hid her face in her hands.

Rocky's gaze lingered on her, she could feel his regard. But the seconds ticked past and eventually he stood, prepared the teapot, brought out sugar, and fetched cream from the icebox.

Her hankie was soiled. She needed a dry one...but that would require standing, climbing the stairs...

"Why would Father flaunt sinful behavior before his flock?" She fought to control her breathing, to slam the flood gates shut.

"I don't know, sweetheart. I don't know."

Water splashed into the teapot as he poured from the kettle.

She didn't deserve him.

The tea steeped as she stared out the window at vivid colors awash in sunlight.

"For your sake," he said at last, "I wish your father had told you himself. Face to face." Bitterness hardened his words, but Rocky's love and respect for Father were there too. "W.W. Stuart should have warned you."

Why *hadn't* W.W. told her about this development? They were friends, weren't they? He'd had the opportunity. But professional men kept their word and never spoke out of turn.

"You're so good to me." She smiled at him, loving his protectiveness. "I think Father did try. Oh, he never told me he had...about that woman..."

Her throat filled again, the tightness making it impossible to speak. But Rocky, bless his generous heart, didn't rush her. "Near the end, when Father somehow knew his time was at hand, he told me—"

This time the tears fell, too easily, and she

resented her weakness. Her hankie, sopping and useless, was no good. Rocky was quick to fetch a stack of clean hankies from a dresser drawer in Mother's upstairs room.

Without saying a word, he set his offering before her and turned to the teapot.

She *really* didn't deserve him.

"I'm not suggesting you should do anything differently," he said, his back to her as he poured tea. "If circumstances brought one of my brothers into my path, we'd be strangers with no connection other than scraps of memories and a blood tie. Yet I'd want to know him."

Contrition immediately swamped her. Rocky was as alone in the world as she. All they had was each other and the realization compounded her guilt. She truly should remember to care about him.

"You might regret not speaking with her while you have the chance." He spooned sugar into the teacup, just the way she liked it.

Strong, callused hands set cup and saucer on the table before her, then settled on her shoulders. She loved it when he touched her this way, as if they faced the world and all its challenges, side by side.

He squeezed, gently massaging the tight muscles of her shoulders. "I imagine she'll leave town on the next train."

"I know." She tasted the steaming tea. Even in the heat of the July day, the beverage soothed from first sip.

"I want her to leave." Not her finest moment,

admitting to the uncharitable, gut-twisting refusal to do what her father asked.

Rocky's gaze rested on her profile. Horrified, embarrassed, shocked at her own behavior, she couldn't look him in the eye.

She'd done the one thing she'd never imagined possible.

She'd disobeyed her father.

FELICITY had never been so angry in her entire life. She might not want a monetary inheritance from her father, but she did want answers.

The father she'd wondered about, made up stories about, excused upon occasion, *waited for*, was a preacher?

Let him suffer the fires of Hell.

He'd sent his attorney to fetch her here, after he was conveniently dead and wouldn't have to face her, hear her list of grievances, nor answer questions.

And that Mr. Gideon, who'd offered her money for room and board. He'd looked her squarely in the eye. A decent man. He'd been the diplomat, plying the answer about Cartwright's ordination from Temperance and the attorney.

The memory of him extending a dollar to her, urging her to take it, proved his mettle.

All wool and a yard wide. Quality. Best there was. Shoulders broad and sturdy enough to bear the weight of the world.

She didn't want *his* money, either.

If she knew where to find him, she'd ask him to explain whatever he knew about the man who'd fathered her.

Aggravated, she wandered the deeply rutted streets of Mountain Home. Though relatively dry now, the hard-packed roads showed evidence of heavy runoff from snow melting in the impressive Rocky Mountains shielding the valley.

The town proved larger and more established than she would have imagined. Nothing like St. Louis, true. But most businesses and residences were frame constructs, many had two stories, and plenty were built of brick. Shops of every kind, industry supporting the mining business, a sawmill, gristmill, liveries and blacksmiths, schools and churches. Two hotels, spaced some distance apart.

She wandered past residences with gardens in full bloom, vegetables ripening and fruit trees showing promise of an eventual harvest.

She bypassed the Catholic church and noted a white steeple visible between rooftops and eventually found herself a good distance behind her father's white clapboard church, punctuated with stained glass windows.

In the cemetery.

Late morning sunlight heated the vegetation and birdsong floated on the breeze as she wandered and eventually found an expensive and large headstone identifying Mrs. Annelise Cartwright's grave. A double headstone stood sentinel to the left of Mrs. Cartwright's, and a single, fresh grave to the right bore a simple wooden cross lashed together with twine.

He'd died only six days earlier. No doubt, a fancy stone with his name carved into it would mark this place when the stonemason completed it.

Nothing but the best for this couple. Had her father married for his wife's money? Was that why Mother had been good enough to compromise but not good enough to wed?

Grass had been carefully trimmed about the tombstones. Not all plots were tended and lovingly cared for, but the Cartwrights' were. Bundles of freshly cut yellow roses, tied with blue ribbon, rested on each of the four graves.

The double headstone next to Mrs. Cartwright's remembered eleven-year-old twin sons, Radford Dunmore Cartwright and Cedric "Ricky" Dunmore Cartwright. *Twin brothers. Beloved sons. Together in life, united in death.* They'd perished in 1874, just five years ago, one day apart. The marker bore four lines of poetry expressing the love of parents.

Why had she been surprised to find Cartwright had married and raised a family? Meeting his daughter had been a shock. Seeing the resting places of his sons and wife made them real.

Cartwright had loved his other children deeply.

The realization shouldn't hurt.

Pain seared through her breast, lodged in her throat, and stoked her anger.

After twenty-five years, *nothing* about the man should have the power to wound her.

She'd never met him. He'd not so much as seen her, at least not that she knew of. And until the attorney fetched her from St. Louis, she hadn't so much as known his name.

Regrets swelled. "Why didn't you contact me while you yet lived? *Why*?"

The breeze teased through the trees at the edges of the graveyard. Birds twittered. But no answer came.

In the near distance, a woman approached, carrying a watering can in one hand and a parasol in the other. Blocking the sun from her eyes with a hand, Felicity recognized Temperance headed directly for her, glowing golden and fair by morning's harsh light. The woman evidently took after her mother.

Or perhaps their father. How would she know?

Felicity had no desire to remain. "I'll go."

Temperance's approach faltered, less than fifteen feet away. "Please."

Please...what? Please go?

With a brief nod, she glanced once more at the earth covering Cedric Cartwright's remains and turned toward the gate.

"Please—stay." Temperance's voice trembled.

Felicity hesitated.

"You shouldn't have to leave." Temperance

rushed on, "All are welcome to pay respects."

No matter how circumspect she kept her behavior, no matter she and Mother had been model citizens of their community, church ladies had never been friendly.

Yet Temperance's simple statement was devoid of malice.

Felicity met the younger woman's gaze and nodded. She'd stay. A few minutes more, to show she wasn't afraid of this half-sister.

Temperance knelt beside Cartwright's grave. She tugged off her pristine white gloves and brushed fingertips over the damp earth—an odd gesture.

This unknown sister had lived with him, had his guidance, protection, and support. Jealousy crowded in.

Questions lurked. Questions Temperance might answer...if she dared ask.

"I planted wildflowers." Temperance blotted her fingers on the grass. "A carpet of blossoms will return each year near the anniversary of his death."

A nice sentiment. She would have nodded, but Temperance hadn't glanced up. She tipped her watering can, tending the wildflower seeds.

Heat from the midday sun burned through Felicity's clothing. Though ample trees had been planted a decade or more ago by settlers, little shade could be found at this hour. Her empty stomach churned. Supper would be served at six o'clock at the boarding house. She'd survive until then.

"You look like him." Temperance rose, pulled

gently at a chain about her neck and withdrew a golden locket from within her bodice. A fine piece of jewelry that must've cost a pretty penny. She slipped a thumbnail between the halves of the locket. Inside, two miniatures.

Felicity couldn't help herself. She moved close enough to see the photographs. The scent of roses, soap, and clothing dried in the sunshine melded, lingering about Temperance.

But Felicity's attention riveted on the likenesses within the locket. A man—supposedly the face of Cedric Cartwright—on the left, and a fair-haired woman on the right.

Young, both of them, vibrant in youth. Probably wedding portraits.

Felicity's gut cramped, even as she took in every feature of her father's face. Recognition stirred, familiar, like looking in a mirror.

Cedric Cartwright had been handsome. Square jaw, high cheekbones, medium-toned hair—probably brown—and clear, light eyes. Good humor lurked about his proper unsmiling mouth and sparkled in his eyes.

No wonder Mother had fancied herself in love.

Drawn to the other image, Felicity examined the face of the woman who'd won Cedric Cartwright's heart. The woman he'd married, shared his life with, raised a family of daughter and sons.

All he'd denied Mother.

Emotion engulfed her. She pressed a hand over her mouth. She would *not* shed tears over this man.

Slowly, as if afraid to move too quickly, Temperance closed her locket and let it fall against her bosom. Her hand came to rest on Felicity's back.

Warm. Soothing. Gentle.

Distressing.

A sob threatened escape.

With long strides, Felicity hurried beyond the cemetery gate and onto the path before the tears fell.

Chapter Four

"Avoid the evil vice of gossip, especially in one you
would select for your lifelong companion. Such a wife
will cause contention wherever she goes and will
nowise bring peace to your home."
~ *The Gentleman's Guide to Courtship and Marriage*

BY EARLY afternoon, Rocky finally broke away from
his duties to call on Miss Felicity Percival. He'd sent a
man to verify she'd taken a room at Ihnken's
Boardinghouse.

He left Mars at the hitching post.

Mrs. Ihnken answered his knock. "Mr. Gideon,
what a surprise to find you on my doorstep. Do come

in, won't you?"

"Thank you, ma'am." He removed his hat, stepped over the threshold and into the front hall. "I'm here to see Miss Percival."

The middle-aged woman's expression soured in an instant. "You don't want to be associating with the likes of her, Mr. Gideon."

Irritation chafed at the *kibitzers*—gossipers—including Mrs. Ihnken.

"No good," she muttered, "No good will come from you so much as *talking* to that woman."

That woman.

The Reverend Cartwright's illegitimate daughter. A brave, determined, hardy soul who'd shown remarkable resiliency.

Oy gevalt! Calming his temper, Rocky offered a congenial smile. "Miss Percival is the sister of my intended, Mrs. Ihnken. I've come to offer my assistance in seeing her returned to her home."

Mrs. Ihnken's nose wrinkled with distaste. She made no move to call Felicity down.

"You would like to see Miss Percival out from under your roof, wouldn't you?"

"She *is* a paying customer."

Tainted, but paying. "If doing so will soothe your worries, Mrs. Ihnken, I'll see you're properly compensated, until Miss Percival departs on the train. She may determine to leave today or stay a while. I cannot say."

"Well..."

If *schmeer* on the *bubbe's* palm made this

easier... He pulled coin from his pocket, selected enough to make the favor worth her while, and pressed it into her cupped hand.

Rocky accepted the seat Mrs. Ihnken offered. He listened to the ticking of the grandfather clock and the old woman's heavy tread on the staircase while he waited. The parlor was comfortably furnished, though showing signs of wear.

Mrs. Ihnken halted on the second story at the rooms for let. Her words carried quite clearly as she raised her voice to call to Miss Percival—too loud for the barrier of a closed bedroom door. The house creaked as footfalls descended *from the attic*, then moved down the main staircase.

He ground his molars and barely resisted swearing.

The attic.

In *July.*

The space must be hot as an oven come noon, a furnace by sundown, and impossible to sleep in by midnight.

In this high mountain valley, *hot* wasn't the same kind of hot as on the plains, but why had the old *bubbe* stowed a paying customer beneath the eaves?

As the owner of the most productive mine in the region, he was well-apprised of places the newcomers roosted. Some pitched tents in fair weather, others bunked in the company's dormitory near the mine. A variety of small cabins and frame houses were rented to families.

If Mrs. Ihnken had ever *once* had a full house, Rocky would be surprised.

Feh! He should have insisted Felicity Percival take his *gelt*—money.

Had Felicity asked for room and board in trade for work? If she'd bartered scrubbing floors for the *privilege* of baking in the attic, he'd—

What?

He'd do something. That was for sure.

If this meeting went differently than expected and Felicity intended to stay in town for one day or one year, he'd make darn sure Mrs. Ihnken had the coin *and* motivation to house Miss Percival in the best room in the house, even if that meant booting another lodger.

He rose to his feet as the women approached the parlor door. Mrs. Ihnken gestured for her boarder to enter, then lumbered toward her kitchen.

No way would he give the old woman more to *kibitz* about. Everyone knew full well she loved nothing more than to share secrets over the garden fence, to the green grocer, to friends who stopped by. The woman had no scruples, and for Temperance's sake, he wouldn't allow her to overhear one word.

"Good afternoon, Miss Percival." He tried to smile—but the hair about Felicity's face was damp, clinging to skin glowing with perspiration. Her calico dress seemed wilted, and the healthy tan of her complexion flushed.

He battled the urge to fist his hands. He'd be back, all right. No way would Miss Percival spend another moment in the attic.

"Mr. Gideon." She nodded a polite greeting.

"I have a matter of business to discuss. Let us retire to the shade of the garden where it's cooler."

"Business?"

The woman's every thought was plain as day, telegraphed for anyone to see. She thought he'd come to strong-arm her into relinquishing her claim to the Cartwright inheritance.

Forcing tension from his face and the set of his shoulders, he spun his hat in his hands. "Nothing to worry about." He tipped his head toward the back of the house, indicating her hostess's big ears and even bigger mouth.

Recognition flashed. "Certainly, Mr. Gideon."

He held the door for her and followed her toward the side garden and shady west side of the house. But less than fifteen steps from the front porch he noticed the perspiration gluing her bodice to her back. Either she'd soaked through a dozen layers of feminine underthings, or she'd eschewed most of it, corset included, to battle the heat.

She *needed* fluids.

The meat of their conversation would have to wait for privacy. *After* she'd had something to eat and drink.

"Let's walk and talk, Miss. I'm thirsty. The bakery down the street offers cold beverages and a variety of sweets."

The mere absence of protestation told him too much.

Feh! Mrs. Ihnken would hear from him, no matter this interview's results.

They walked in silence for a few minutes, the sun hot on his back. His hat shaded him from the worst of the glare, but Miss Percival had no bonnet and therefore no shade. Her sun-kissed skin told him she typically worked outside without benefit of a hat and that bothered him.

"You've come to ensure I leave town, and forfeit claim to Miss Cartwright's inheritance."

Her blunt statement confirmed his suspicions. "That's up to you, ma'am."

"Your interests lie with Miss Cartwright."

No argument there.

"The will stated what would happen to the Cartwright house if I stay, but not if I leave. Will Miss Cartwright's claim on the property be uncontested if I leave and refuse the confounded stipulations?"

He liked the idea that Miss Percival wanted to see the property safe in Temperance's keeping. "I don't know for certain. I haven't studied law."

"I meant what I said. I don't want the old man's money or his house. I'll be on the train, within the week."

Interesting. With daily trains through Mountain Home, why would she stay even one more day? What did she want? "You're sure you want to leave?"

They passed by three matrons clustered about the grocer's entrance. Rocky nodded, touching the brim of his hat in respect. Mrs. McGillicudy—usually nice enough—turned quickly to the other two to whisper. *Kibitzers.*

"I'm sure." Felicity ignored the women with well-practiced aplomb.

"That's part of what I want to discuss." He checked the traffic, then touched her lower back to escort her across the rutted dirt road. He'd been right. Soaked through and no corset. Worse, knobby bones of her spine protruded.

He couldn't help drawing comparisons. Temperance never left the house without appropriate attire, including gloves and hat. She'd never think of going without all the frippery women wore beneath their dresses. And never missed a meal in her life.

Miss Felicity's profile, however, showed off the Cartwright high cheekbones in stark relief. She'd be prettier twenty pounds heavier.

Not to say that she wasn't pretty just as she was.

The Reverend Cartwright had been a handsome fellow, and both his daughters were lovely. Different, one dark and one fair, but lovely just the same. The Cartwright boys had been attractive lads.

But back to the point at hand.

Where had he been? Oh, yes. Money.

He cleared his throat, nodded at Mr. Nance exiting the bakery. He took Felicity's elbow, urging her to halt. "I can't think of a way to say what I need to say without offending you, so I'll just say it. You don't look like you can buy a train ticket home. Did Mr. Stuart provide one?"

Surprise flitted across her features, chased hard and fast with disappointment, then anger. He saw the moment she shut down hard. "That's none of your concern."

He held up a hand in a placating gesture. "Just listen, all right? You're my intended's sister. You say you don't want Cartwright's money—but if you're stranded here and need a train ticket, I'm the one to buy it."

He'd seen her assessing his worth by the cut of his clothes, the newness of his boots, the expense of his hat. Unfortunately, he'd done the same to her.

"You want me out of town, away from your lady."

"Ma'am, if it were any business of mine, I'd urge you to stay. You and Temperance have just found each other and barely exchanged five words. I'd like to see you two talk, determine if you can be friends." Temperance might not understand all she poised to give up, but he did.

"Why?"

Candid. Plainspoken. Curious. He liked that in a woman.

"Family connections are valuable, a treasure. Look, I lost track of my brothers so long ago, I hardly remember them. I'd give my fortune to reunite with them."

She tipped her head, considering his response. "You know something. About me or Cedric Cartwright's reasons for summoning me."

His gut lurched, every muscle in his abdomen tighter than a hangman's knot.

"Don't deny it. I saw your expression in the

lawyer's office last night."

No way would he disclose all that, not on the street with ears everywhere and the gossip mill already churning. "Come in out of the sun. Let's get us a cold drink and a big slice of bread."

He opened the door and nudged her inside. The bakery, awash in homey scents of cinnamon and vanilla, sugar and yeast, baking cakes and sweet pies, was just as warm as outside. But the lack of direct sun was pleasant as could be.

Eight or ten people sat dining at the clusters of tables and chairs but no one was in line, denying Felicity the opportunity to press for answers. The proprietor, newlywed Thaddeus Whipple, staffed the counter, and Rocky placed their orders. When Miss Felicity didn't complain about his selections, he paid and they took the one empty table.

Rocky set her plate before her, a big slice of dark wheat bread with melted cheese on top. One more trip for tall glasses of iced tea. "Sugar?" He removed the lid from the sugar bowl and offered it.

She tasted her tea, then stirred in a heaping spoonful as young Mrs. Whipple moved about the tables, clearing plates and accepting compliments from their patrons.

Felicity Percival wasn't distracted by the commotion, the tall glass of sweet tea, or the yeasty aroma of the meal before her. She hadn't forgotten, not for one moment, the question she'd asked.

"Eat. Drink. When you're done, we'll go to my office." He glanced about the busy dining area, ensuring she'd catch his meaning. Too many ears. "I'll tell you everything I know. Then *you* decide whether you stick around or accept my offer for a train ticket anywhere you want to go and on any day you choose."

Chapter Five

"Once your choice of brides is made with cool and deliberate confidence, see that you are not lured away from that chosen one."

~ The Gentleman's Guide to Courtship and Marriage

HE BELONGS to Temperance Cartwright.

Felicity forced her attention away from Mr. Gideon, though sunlight illuminated streaks of fire in his dark brown hair, and intelligence shone in the warmth of his chocolate eyes.

She blinked, drained her tea, and finished the last bite of heavy bread and melted cheese. She would ignore him. She would. And concentrate on her stomach, full to bursting. She'd not eaten so well in ages.

Breakfast that morning had been a single flapjack, a few chunks of fried potato, and one strip of bacon. Two male boarders had been served hearty meals quadruple the size.

Perhaps the old woman found a lady's appetite decidedly vulgar.

More likely she'd heard about the circumstances of Felicity's birth. As usual, her money wasn't as good as everyone else's.

The contrast between mean old Mrs. Ihnken treatment and Mr. Rocky Gideon's kindhearted decency stood out in sharp relief.

The man was uncommonly good. And fundamentally appealing.

If and when she ever found a man who could see past her flaws and love her...she hoped he strongly resembled Mr. Gideon.

She drew a deep breath, wiped her fingers on the napkin and prepared to rise.

Mr. Gideon moved quickly, surprisingly so for such a big man, and held her chair.

She shouldn't be surprised. He'd shown himself to be in possession of manners.

She wouldn't take it personally. He'd likely hold a door or chair or carry a parcel for any female in town, even mean Mrs. Ihnken. Or a girl born in shame.

Even the unwanted, unknown, illegitimate sister of the woman he'd soon wed.

Oh, yes. She'd be wise to remember. Just because he was the first to hold her chair, the only man to look her in the eye and offer support and help and options didn't mean he saw her as anything but a problem for his intended bride.

A shameful, hidden secret.

"Thank you, Mr. Gideon, for—" Luncheon? Kindness? Decent treatment? "—the meal. The tea was particularly refreshing."

"You're welcome, Miss Percival." He opened the door for her, then did the most surprising, most alarming thing yet. He offered her his arm and refused to let her ignore it.

So she took that proffered courtesy, slipping her hand through the crook of his elbow and allowed him to escort her around the corner and down the street.

Past shopkeepers, fine ladies and gentlemen, honest ranchers and their upstanding wives. In front of God, neighbors, and everyone.

Despite the fact the rumor mill would soon inform Miss Temperance Cartwright she'd been on his arm.

And seated with him at luncheon.

The *one* thing she would never allow the rumor mill to pass along was her most inappropriate pleasure in the company of her half-sister's intended husband.

Oh, no. She would not tarnish herself or him. And she would *never* fall for a man she couldn't have.

Inside the cool building of *R.V. Gideon & Co.*, her eyes adjusted to the comparable dimness as Mr.

Gideon excused a few employees from the outer office. "Take the rest of the day off, gentlemen. My treat. Enjoy the sunshine."

The well-dressed fellows thanked Mr. Gideon, collected hats and canes, and hurried through the door.

She should have been uncomfortable when Mr. Gideon turned the key in the lock, but he'd shown her impeccable manners and gave her no reason to fear.

He led her into his personal office in the back of the building and seated her in an upholstered chair. The richly appointed room, with handsome wainscoting, framed paintings hanging on either side of heavy draperies at the windows, and a chandelier of five oil lamps hanging from the ceiling above a massive mahogany desk, was furnished with an array of chairs for guests.

Maybe not guests. Businessmen. Investors. Perhaps competitors.

Last night, Mr. Gideon had been dressed in a costly suit of clothes, a heavy gold watch-fob dangling from his waistcoat. Today, he wore the rough, durable clothes of a laborer. "What business are you in, Mr. Gideon?"

"Call me Rocky."

His formal name maintained boundaries.

"Please." Instead of sitting behind the desk, he took a seat near her and turned it to provide an intimate proximity. "We're soon to be family. No need for formality."

She nodded, but had no intention of addressing

him if doing so required use of his given name.

"Mining. I own the Peerless Mine, one of the two largest and most productive gold and silver mines in the area."

"Oh." Her modest, serviceable calico turned to rags in this opulent room. Compared to the lawyer's office, this room's furnishings must have cost double. This office building, from roof to carpets, draperies to paintings, furnishings to carved marble mantelpiece defined Mr. Gideon's import, power, and wealth.

Whatever he wanted, he'd obtain.

This prominent, prosperous man wanted Temperance Cartwright. He belonged to Temperance, and she to him.

Felicity vowed, then and there, to rip out her undesirable attraction to this man by the roots. She controlled her passions. Her passions did not control her.

So with a deep breath and a conscious effort to relax into the comfortable chair, she met her host's brown eyes, warm with compassion.

"I believe we're safe from prying ears, Mr. Gideon. Do tell what great secret couldn't be overheard by the good people of Mountain Home."

"I'LL MAKE you a deal, Miss Percival," Rocky said to

Felicity, ignoring the *kvetching* of his conscience. "You solemnly promise to address me as Rocky and I'll answer every question you have about your father, his frame of mind, his decisions. Everything."

Hints of her thoughts played over her marvelously expressive face. Doubt. Concern. Effort to determine what he wanted from her.

"First, my offer for a train ticket stands." No sense mentioning the bill at Mrs. Ihnken's. Correcting her room assignment would be his little gift. "When you determine it's time to go, your fare is covered. I'll leave money with the stationmaster."

"Why?"

"Because your father or his attorney should have secured your return tickets."

"They preferred I stay." Evidently, she wondered why he wanted her to leave town.

"I'll make this easy, Miss Felicity. Like I said, it's your decision whether you stay or go. If you want to go, know I can easily afford it."

She blinked, evidently uncomfortable.

"This isn't about the money. It's about honoring your choice in the matter. Like I said, I hope you decide to stay."

Something odd and a little reminiscent of hope or pleasure flickered through her imperfect gray eyes. In the indirect light, they appeared more hazel than gray.

"You asked a loaded question," he reminded her. "You want to know what I know about your father, what was on my mind last night in Stuart's office. I'll tell you because it's best you know the whole truth. It's also best for Temperance, and I want everything best for her. I want to do the right thing."

Felicity watched him closely, as if weighing his words. She must have reached a favorable conclusion for she offered a small smile. "Very well, Rocky. You must call me Felicity."

With pleasure.

"I recognize," she said, "my appearance brought tremendous embarrassment to your fiancée."

"I'm courting Temperance," he clarified, not sure why it mattered, "but we're not yet engaged to be married."

She shifted in her chair, uncomfortable. "Please tell me what you know."

"Felicity," he called her by name because she'd given him leave to do so and her name on his tongue brought him *mechaye*—pleasure. "Your sister is not embarrassed, not by you. Angry that your shared father aired dirty laundry, yes, but she's *rutzer*." Young and without experience. "She'll have a change of heart."

"What language is it you toss in here and there? You use words I don't understand."

He hadn't realized. "It's Yiddish—Jewish."

"I'm surprised Cartwright would allow his daughter to wed a Jew."

He chuckled and noted her tension waned. "I arrived in Mountain Home when a teenager—just coming into my height, and without family. I needed work, a place to stay, someone who'd treat me right.

Cedric Cartwright went out of his way to place me with Mikkel Herschstein who happens to be Jewish. Mick became like a father, or maybe an older brother. But Mick and Cedric decided I was born a Christian, best I knew, and I should remain a Christian."

"Ah." Her expression grew pensive.

Leaning forward in his chair, he rested elbows upon his knees and caught a hint of her scent. Clean woman beneath honest sweat, sunshine, and a fragrance all her own. Awareness tingled up his spine and traveled all the way to his fingertips.

Not the way he ought to notice his future sister-in-law.

"It seems," she said, "Cartwright knew of my existence for some time, yet he made no attempt to contact me until after his death. I must have been an embarrassment."

"He was *not* embarrassed by you, Felicity."

She shook her head, adamant. Fine dark hairs had escaped the knot at the back of her head and floated free. "What other reason could there possibly be?"

She clearly doubted his ability to comprehend the minister's state of mind.

"I wish I knew, precisely, why he didn't contact you. All I can do is guess." How could he help her understand? "Indulge me for a moment, will you?"

Several seconds of intense eye contact passed before she nodded.

"I recall little of my parents," he confided. "My mother wept all the time and nothing I did comforted her." He'd lived with it for most of his life and could speak of it without emotion. "She left one day and never looked back. She walked away from sons. I don't recall how many. And left our father too. I have no idea why. Mother's selfishness, and maybe my father's, destroyed their marital happiness, ripped our family to shreds, and scattered their sons to the four winds."

"I'm sorry."

Why hadn't he yet shared much of this with his future bride? He ought to.

"Once, I asked a man at the orphanage when my father would come for me." The memory remained as vivid and painful as it had been in his youth. "I must have been four or five. The stern fellow's expression was devoid of hope. He left me wondering what I'd done so wrong that my father abandoned me."

Passion fired in her eyes, warming gray to near-blue. "You did nothing wrong. A child is not responsible for his parents' happiness."

He couldn't help but chuckle. This woman, defending him?

He reached for her hand, savored the warmth and roughness of her fingers. "I'll admit, it took years, well into adulthood, but I figured it out. The deficiency resided in my parents, not me."

"You're right."

He smiled at her. A strange, moving sensation washed through him. Had he actually met someone much like himself? Two people cut from the same bolt of cloth. A matched set.

She *understood.*

He wanted nothing more than to remain like this, her hand in his. Whatever he told her, he knew she'd understand without judgment.

Feh!

How had he allowed a flicker of attraction for Temperance's sister to flash from simple appreciation to...to *this*?

No. He could not, would not deviate from his chosen path.

He knew what he wanted. Temperance. *Temperance* would be his wife. His perfect helpmate. After all, he'd carefully selected her. He'd courted her with the precise purpose of falling so deeply in love that their marriage would last.

It had been too long since he'd spent an evening courting his intended. With the sudden loss of her father, the funeral, and the shocking news of her half-sister, he'd neglected his love. He wouldn't repeat that mistake.

He *needed* stability.

He drew a deep breath and gathered his sanity. He would remain in control. "You," he whispered, "are not responsible for the deficiencies of your parents."

She squeezed his hand then slipped her fingers free. She must've realized she'd given too much away for her expression was blank, a slate wiped clean. "I never believed I was."

Chapter Six

"Understand the importance of choosing with your intellect and not your heart. If your heart be not encumbered elsewhere, you will come to love the one you have chosen. No man ever loved a woman—no, not one—without first determining that she was indeed the right one for him to love."
~ *The Gentleman's Guide to Courtship and Marriage*

"GOOD." HE shifted on his chair. "I remember the day The Reverend Cartwright learned about you. I was present."

Felicity flinched.

He wanted to recapture her hand, soothe her.

Instead, he balled two fists. "It so happened I was at Murphy's Mercantile, picking up my mail. Your father was distressed by the return address on a letter."

Felicity watched him with intent, as if taking in every nuance of the story revealed in his expression and his posture. He forced his fists to unfurl.

"He opened the letter immediately, sat down heavily on the bench outside the store, and began reading. Tears streamed down his face as he read. He wept openly, shamelessly, as if his heart were breaking. I couldn't ignore him, so I sat."

Rocky remembered the tug of emotion as if that summer's day had been last week. "He did the oddest thing. He handed me the letter. I hesitated, of course. A fellow doesn't read another man's private mail. But he nodded at me as he blew his nose, so I did as he asked and read it."

"From my mother?"

"Yes." Word for word, that brief letter had branded his memory.

"When did he learn about me?"

"Summer, two years ago. I'm not sure precisely. Late May, I think."

She pressed a hand over her mouth. Her eyes widened, and for several seconds he thought she'd weep. What had happened to her or her mother to incite that revelatory letter?

He ached to reach for her, but knew that would be foolish. He wanted to ask questions but held back.

By degrees, she regained control. "I don't

understand." Her voice sounded high and tight. "Why would the minister show you the letter and not Temperance?"

"He must have—" believed he protected her? Thought the timing wrong? Thought he had one more day, until death stole the opportunity? "We had an unusual bond. A close friendship."

Pain flickered across her features. Regret charged in. Why hadn't he censured his words? Of course Felicity would be hurt by his cavalier reference to unusual bonds and close friendships—she would have wanted those things with her father.

"I apologize, Felicity." He took her hand, squeezed it in earnestness. "I spoke without thinking. Can you forgive me?"

Her gaze locked on their joined hands. Her bowed head hid her expressions, denied him clues to her thoughts. But she didn't pull away, her work-toughened fingers warm against his palm.

"There is nothing to forgive." Her voice sounded small. "Mother wrote because she'd taken ill. Cancer, the doctor said. She died in June, two years past."

Rocky had Felicity's hand halfway to his mouth before he caught himself. Not wise, but compassion overrode judgment. He pressed a kiss to her knuckles.

He knew the ache of loneliness. The darkness that encroached without family and home.

He tugged his chair closer and with his elbow on his knee, kept her hand clutched in his own. She needed him, needed his touch, he knew it and apparently so did she for she didn't pull away.

"What did Mother write?"

"Her letter was brief. She informed the pastor that she'd borne him a daughter nine months after he'd departed St. Louis, she'd named you Felicity, and true to your name, you'd filled her life with joy."

"I wondered how he knew my name."

W.W. Stuart's arrival in St. Louis must have come as a surprise—both dreadful and wonderful. He could imagine the mixed feelings he'd experience if he ever found his father.

She'd taken his hand in both of hers, holding on the way a little child clutches the hand of a parent. But then her thumb caressed his pinkie and he instantly revised that assumption. This was no platonic hand-holding.

"I don't know whether to be more upset with Mother or Cartwright," she murmured. "I was with my mother every day until the end. She could have told me." She met his gaze then, her hands stilling. Tears pooled in her eyes but did not spill. "All she ever told me about my father was that she'd loved him and he'd loved her. Hopelessly in love, Mother said. But she refused to confess his name. No stories, no pictures, no details. If Mr. Stuart hadn't found me at the boardinghouse, I'd never have known."

"I'm sorry you found out this way." He remembered her shock and panic upon learning Cartwright had married and borne children. "Cartwright should have prepared Temperance. And he should have contacted you himself." No matter how much Rocky had admired and respected the man, he'd made a horrible mistake by leaving the revelation to W.W. Stuart and his will. Waning health, cough or no cough, some things had to be done.

"Any guesses why?"

"I expect he knew the news would hurt Mrs. Cartwright and Temperance, though his—" what word could he possibly use? "—love for your mother occurred prior to his marriage. Mrs. Cartwright hadn't been well for quite some time, and not long after the letter arrived she took to her bed. She passed away last winter."

She nodded. Her grip tightened on his hand.

"I suppose he thought he had time, after his wife passed. He probably clung to the idea of tomorrow." He held her gaze, sensed their mutual understanding. Cartwright had been a fool to fritter away time he could have had with this remarkable woman, his daughter. "He procrastinated until it was too late."

THE FOLLOWING evening, Rocky made it a point to court Temperance. Seven days had elapsed since her father's sudden death. So much had happened in that week: the shock of Pastor Cartwright's passing, the visitation, burial, a half-sister's arrival in town and reading of the will.

And, worst of all, Rocky's inconvenient, highly improper attraction to Felicity.

Tonight *would* fix things.

Time in Temperance's company, wholly focused on her, would correct his errors in judgment. He'd get back on track, remember all the reasons he'd chosen Temperance to become his wife and set about courting her with full intent of falling madly in love.

Yes, this evening's courting would solidify his affection for his chosen bride and all would be well again.

He pushed the porch swing into motion, loving the sensation of sitting quietly with her, sharing conversation, sipping ice-cold lemonade, and in no hurry. Courting at home, per the minister's advice, was truly ideal.

Without distraction of a theater production, company of friends, or time spent driving, they had nothing to worry about but each other.

An occasional pedestrian or wagon rumbled past in the heat of the setting sun. In full view of neighbors and townspeople, no one could fret about inappropriate behavior.

Inappropriate behavior...Rocky's thoughts rebounded to Felicity. For the hundredth time.

He didn't know whether to hope she'd departed on this afternoon's train or pray she hadn't. Now that she'd found the answers she'd sought, she might leave at any time.

True to his word, he'd left money in the stationmaster's keeping. And paid a visit to stingy Mrs. Ihnken.

Widow Ihnken had firmed her lips, pouted, complained, accepted his *gelt*, and vowed to move Miss Percival from the attic to the large corner bedroom with two windows so she might enjoy the cross-breeze.

"If she shows her true colors and tempts my male boarders, I'll put her out."

"You'll do no such thing."

"I will. I don't care if you're a wealthy man, Mr. Gideon. I don't care if our dearly departed minister was to be your father-in-law, I won't tolerate sin under my roof."

Interesting that the harpy blamed Felicity for the accident of her birth but withheld judging the man who, by his own admission, fathered her.

He should be pleased Mrs. Ihnken's respect for the pastor hadn't diminished, but the insult to Felicity was offensive.

"Rocky?" Temperance touched his arm, the cold of her lemonade glass transferred to her hand, seeping through his shirtsleeve. Blast the intolerable heat for making it difficult to fasten his attentions where they belonged.

"I'm sorry, my dear. Beg pardon. My mind wandered."

"You seem troubled. Won't you tell me what distracts you so?"

By tacit agreement, they'd not spoken of her

half-sister. Why tarnish their cherished time together? "It's nothing."

She eyed him closely, assessing. "Won't you share your thoughts?"

Wasn't this intimacy, sharing private thoughts and ideas, what courtship was all about? He couldn't admit he'd been plagued by constant reflection upon Felicity. He scrambled to find something—*anything*—factual, truthful, that would have otherwise weighed heavily upon him. "Production is waning. And today I lost three men in a cave-in."

"Oh, Rocky. I hadn't heard."

"I didn't want to worry you."

"I know, and I'm grateful. Yet how can I comfort you if I'm unaware?"

He'd have to learn to share his concerns, especially once they married. Temperance had a gift for lightening his burden.

She brushed her fingertips over his cheek. Her touch felt remarkably good. "Thank you, sweetheart."

"Let's talk of something more pleasant, shall we?" For the briefest of moments, she rested her cheek against his shoulder. He wished she'd linger, wished she'd show him as much affection as he tried to lavish on her. "The plans for Founders' Day are coming along nicely."

She'd kept him well-informed over the past many months. Her work on the committee for the twentieth anniversary had been interrupted by the pastor's illness and passing, but she must've met with the ladies again. That was good. "I'm glad to hear it."

"The parade will be bigger and better than ever before. Donations for fireworks are nearly half again more generous than last year. It will be quite a show."

Naturally, she expected him to accompany her. He wouldn't miss it. One of the benefits of a courtship like theirs.

He nudged the swing into motion as she filled him in on the plans, the developments, and for several minutes, the pall of grief lifted. She smiled and laughed and he remembered adoring her.

Uh oh...*remembered* adoring her wasn't the target he aimed for.

He rolled his nearly empty glass between his palms and savored her warmth against his side.

See? His determination to focus on Temperance and Temperance alone was working...*mostly*.

At last she finished sharing all the details, rose, and took his glass. "I'll refresh your drink." Her smile reflected the old softness, the gentleness of her sentiment.

She really was the sweetest of young ladies.

She entered the house and he toed the swing back and forth, wishing for a bit of a breeze. Insects hummed and buzzed and worked over the blossoms in the flowerbeds. A mother, somewhere on the block, called to her children to come inside. An older couple strolled along the walk just beyond the picket fence, arm in arm, evidently comfortable in their decades together.

That's what he wanted—longevity and contentment and joy in marriage. Permanence and domestic bliss, conjugal felicity—

Not just felicity, as in happiness. But *Felicity.* The woman.

He wanted...*Felicity.*

Feh!

How many times had he thought of her that very hour? Ten? Twenty? Even while courting his future wife?

Chapter Seven

"Whenever possible, courtship should occur in the home, with the blessing of and complete oversight of the young lady's mother."
~ *The Gentleman's Guide to Courtship and Marriage*

AS IF ROCKY'S yearning conjured Felicity, she appeared.

Strolling up the walk, she greeted the elderly couple, a ready smile upon her lips. Her gaze locked onto his and she sucked in a draught of air.

As if she were as inexplicably drawn to him as he was to her.

No, *no*!

No unwelcome infatuation. *No* disloyal division of affection. His focus should be wholly upon Temperance.

It *was* entirely on Temperance.

The front door shut with the squeak of a hinge. "Darling, your lemonade." She pressed the cold glass into his palm even as he forced his attention from the forbidden and to his chosen love.

His expression surely betrayed him, though he infused as much devotion and tenderness into his smile as possible.

But guilt surged high, drowning his good intentions.

The Reverend Cartwright would have been disappointed—not to mention Mrs. Cartwright, whose approval of Rocky's courtship had meant the world to him. She'd trusted him with her daughter, her greatest prize.

He *must* regain his composure and his loyalty. He *would*.

The moment Temperance noticed her half-sister just beyond the garden fence, her posture stiffened. The light he'd managed to rekindle in her sky-blue eyes extinguished.

Guilt gave way to self-loathing.

He prayed Temperance hadn't sensed that his thoughts clung to her unwanted sister.

He must fix this. *Now.*

Still, beyond the white pickets, Felicity waited. Rocky sensed her longing, her craving for all she saw—but it wasn't covetousness. Just abject loneliness. A need too big to contain. A need to connect with family, to belong, to sip lemonade and be with people who welcomed her.

He comprehended the need in his marrow, soul-deep.

Had she come here intentionally? Seeking companionship or the opportunity to speak to her sister? Yet he'd witnessed her surprise as if she hadn't known which house belonged to the Cartwrights.

No way could he invite the young woman to join them—that was Temperance's choice. Time slipped past and Temperance behaved as though she hadn't seen Felicity.

His heart squeezed at the loneliness etched on Felicity's features. He raised a hand in greeting and smiled at Felicity.

He turned back to Temperance, his objective solid. Disgust with himself kicked hard. How had he become so divided, so torn between the two women?

He sipped, hiding behind his glass. "Delicious as always."

Temperance smiled, but light failed to reach her eyes.

Despite the public space they occupied, he took his love's hand in his, gave her slender, shapely fingers a squeeze. She adored holding hands, and he used this knowledge to his advantage, even as Felicity retreated.

"DO TELL us about Miss Percival." Caroline Finlay's interest seemed ladylike as always.

Temperance didn't feel gracious. "I had no idea she existed until Father's lawyer introduced her." She still hadn't forgiven W.W. for that. She pursed her lips, focusing her attention on the tiny stitches she wove into the quilt's double wedding ring design.

The seven other women paused, glanced to one another, then to Temperance.

"No!"

"Oh, darling."

"He didn't!"

"It's true?"

Shock, surprise, dismay—emotions Temperance had already battled—registered on her friends' faces. Most satisfying and endearing. She'd known attending their sewing circle had been the right thing to do.

"Why is she still in town?" Ann Abbott had been the first to marry from their circle of friends. Her outspokenness had blossomed since.

Enjoying all eyes on her, Temperance lifted one shoulder in a shrug. "Who's to say? She came by last night to get a look at my home while I sat on the porch with my fiancé."

"No!"

"Brazen!"

"What did you do? How did you get through it?"

"Oh, you poor dear."

Celia Jones ran her hand over the bright blue and yellow pattern she'd chosen for the quilt top. This beautiful project was slated for her trousseau. "Mrs. Pettingill said she strongly resembles..." Celia looked up, met Temperance's gaze, and the compassion there blended with something a whole lot like fascination. "Our beloved minister, The Reverend Cartwright—well, it's just so hard to believe."

Temperance pierced her needle through the fabric and woolen batting with more force than necessary.

Father may have chosen to reveal his past to his parishioners, but hadn't he cared what talk would do to *her* good name?

Murmurs of agreement circled the quilt in Celia's parlor. Morning sunlight spilled through east-facing windows and a lovely breeze ruffled the sheer curtains at the windows. Opposite, the door stood open to allow free movement of air.

She ought to defend her father, reinforce his goodness in light of this tragedy, shouldn't she? "Miss Percival is twenty-five years of age." She couldn't bring herself to say more, but hoped they understood his...*mistake*...occurred before his marriage or ordination. "I'm confident my father meant well and acted in keeping with his conscience." If only she understood.

"Are you sure?" Ann asked, doubt still evident

in her tone. "How do you know Miss Percival is your, um..." As if hesitant to employ the term *sister*, she struggled to find a suitable alternative. "...father's daughter?"

"I don't know. Except for Father's word." An itty-bitty white lie.

Because, unfortunately, she *did* know.

Not only had she seen the letter on W.W. Stuart's desk, in the strong, confident hand she would know anywhere, she'd had far too much time to study the woman's physical appearance on three separate occasions. By late evening light both indoors and out. By the direct light of midday sun, her features so closely resembled Father, she couldn't justify denying Miss Percival was indeed her father's daughter.

Pain lanced through her chest, yet again, and she prayed her mother never knew, never so much as wondered.

"We are ever loyal to you, Temperance." Caroline Finlay, also married, was always the voice of reason. Perhaps motherhood had contributed to Caroline's wisdom and compassion for she seemed more level-headed and reasonable every year. "We stand by you."

Murmurs of agreement buoyed Temperance's flagging spirits.

"Thank you, dear friends." She couldn't help the overwhelming rush of affection for these seven closest confidants. They'd been through school together, joys and heartbreaks and challenges. There would be more weddings in the coming months, perhaps three more within the upcoming year, including her own. "Your association has helped me through this trying time."

Along with friends of Mother's, this circle had prepared the repast for the visitation and funeral goers. The wake had seen nearly everyone in the surrounding county paying their respects.

Father had been well-respected and dearly loved. Now, if only that goodwill continued, despite the crisis.

Jennifer Kennedy threaded her needle, intent upon her task. "I saw her out walking last night."

Ah, yes. Strolling by the Cartwright home—the house promised to the usurper if she'd live in harmony with Temperance.

Decidedly un-Christian thoughts paraded through Temperance's head. What did Miss Felicity Percival want? To see Temperance securely wedded to Mr. Rocky Gideon so the home that had been Temperance's all of her life—with her father *and* her mother—would be forfeit to her greedy hands?

Or did Miss Percival take after her mother and wish to cause Temperance more pain...by luring Rocky into sinful paths?

Oh, she'd witnessed his interest and curiosity, his wave and smile in acknowledgment. She'd wanted to scream. Or pull him by both hands into the house and plant him on the sofa with his back toward the street-facing windows. She'd keep him under lock and key if doing so would make one iota of difference.

But Rocky was a headstrong man. She could no

more force him to bend to her will than she could leap over the moon. He worked hard and always achieved his end goal. She should trust him. He'd chosen to court *her* and *always* kept his word.

Feminine voices murmured agreement. In this uncommon heat, it seemed everyone had been outside in the shade, seeking relief from stifling indoor heat. *Must* Miss Percival parade herself about when every eye in town sought a glimpse of her?

The conversation around the quilt had turned to the upcoming Founders' Day Celebration and their sewing circle's plans to enter picnic baskets in the raffle. Temperance couldn't follow the conversation, not with her mind awhirl.

"Temperance?" Jennifer placed a gentle hand upon Temperance's arm. She must've spoken once, already, for the concern in her pale green eyes radiated intense worry. "Did you know," she spoke softly as to not draw attention from the others, "Mr. Gideon escorted Miss Percival from the boardinghouse to Whipple Bakery for luncheon, day before yesterday?"

Panic seared Temperance's insides. She shook her head, mute.

Jennifer's china complexion splotched pink. "I'm sure he's just being kind, for he's such a gentleman. But then he...oh, dear. He uh...escorted her on his arm to his office, the one here in town, not up at the mine. I only tell you this because it wasn't two minutes and he'd shooed everyone out of the building so he might have a private interview with your, um...Miss Percival."

Temperance couldn't speak. Her face flushed, hot and surely reddened. She averted her gaze, fighting to regain her equilibrium.

Her tongue might have seized, turned to granite, but most unladylike epithets rolled through her thoughts. Mother's admonishments followed close behind: *Ladies do not speak profanities, Temperance. You have a delicate position in Mountain Home, and all you say and do reflects upon the minister.*

Bitterness raced through her. *What about the minister's actions reflecting upon her?*

Jennifer remained intent upon Temperance. "I'm sorry."

Oh, please, let her mortification remain hidden!

Jennifer sighed. "I shouldn't have spoken. Your Mr. Gideon's character is above reproach."

With her throat still obstructed, she nodded and returned to her stitching. Rather, pretended to, because tears blurred her vision.

Jennifer was right, of course. Rocky's character *was* stellar. Everyone knew he had no vices: never gambled, did not imbibe, did not associate with loose women, and always—*always*—conducted himself befitting a gentleman. Mother had been certain of his devotion and suitability as a husband.

So had Father.

To doubt him now seemed faithless and hysterical.

Irrational.

Pointless, as she was the one who'd been less...well, less rational. Grief had robbed her good sense these past many months since Mother's passing, stole time and attention and affection away from the goodhearted man her parents approved of.

A desperate urgency to speak to W.W. Stuart arose. She *needed* him. She needed answers.

The attorney had worked closely with Father to manage the estate, prepare the will, arrange for Miss Percival to be present. He'd know Father's state of mind in those last weeks and months. He might understand why Father had left such important, personal revelations to his last will and testament.

The moment she could slip away, she'd go directly to Mr. Stuart.

Chapter Eight

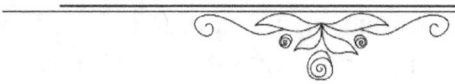

"Permit no disagreement nor offense to come between you and the lady you have selected to become your wife."
~ *The Gentleman's Guide to Courtship and Marriage*

EARLY THURSDAY afternoon, three days after the reading of the will, Rocky returned from The Peerless. He loped into Mountain Home on horseback, covered in mining dust. He rounded the corner to a sight that yanked him up short.

Temperance's sewing circle—not all seven of 'em, but four or five, surrounded Felicity on the side of the road, one block from the boardinghouse.

Menacing postures. Raised voices. A shove. Felicity fell onto her *tuches*. Bottom.

Temperance? Couldn't find her blond head in the melee.

The corseted predators closed in. Were they *mad*?

In that moment, he was a boy again, tormented by anyone bigger or stronger. Lack of decent clothing. Lack of obvious parents. Simple *lack* painted a target on his scrawny back.

Ill-fitting hand-me-downs billowing in the wind, blood flowing from a busted nose, he screamed at the bullies, "I do have a father. And a mama! Just 'cause I don't know where they are don't make 'em less real!"

Long buried abandonment and helplessness erupted, resurged, engulfed him, squeezing air from his lungs. This pack of she-wolves reduced him to that undersized, underfed, unloved pass-around boy no one wanted.

Today, he owned a profitable business, a fortune in the bank and real estate, well-tailored clothing made to *his* measurements, and ten-dollar boots sturdy enough to last two decades.

He was *not* helpless.

He whistled sharply, expecting the fight to break up.

Instead, the pack of petticoated raiders pounced.

He touched his heels to Mars's flanks and charged into battle.

Only two skirted sentries remained standing. Felicity had to be on the bottom of the mob beneath lace-trimmed petticoats, button-up boots, elbows, and feminine shrieks. A squeal preceded a fancy hat rolling away.

Rocky dismounted while Mars was still in motion, grabbed two women by flying arms and yanked them back.

One shrieked, black curls falling out of pins and covering her face.

"Mrs. Abbott." Rocky growled and set the *balabusta* aside. Satisfaction surged as he noted a swelling eye. She thought herself untouchable—and that drove him mad. She was *trouble*. "Fancy meeting you here."

The scuffle seemed to cease all at once. *Finally*.

Half of them stood, half remained prone in the dirt. Felicity, at quick glance, seemed relatively unharmed and madder than a wet hen.

Six females glared at him.

Including Felicity.

He noted a few scratched faces and one woman holding her nose. Several ladies' hair hung askew, pulled from pins. He tried to tamp down his gratification at the sight. Felicity was a fighter. Like him.

"What got into you?" he demanded, glaring first at bossy Mrs. Abbot, then her cohorts in crime. "You think it's a good idea to fistfight in public, *ladies*?"

Lightning struck, sudden and brilliant, and he *knew*.

Oy gevalt!

Temperance.

She might not be in their midst, but somehow, she'd started this.

His adorable, gentle-hearted, Christian woman, who never passed judgment on a soul had somehow informed her friends that Miss Felicity Percival was to be ostracized...and beaten?

Disappointment doused the double-helping of reality.

He offered Felicity a hand and glared until she accepted. He pulled her to her feet.

"Start talking." His thunderous expression worked on his miners and it worked on nutty Ann Abbott.

"Don't pretend," Mrs. Abbott said, somehow looking down her nose at him though he stood a full foot taller, "you don't know what this...*person*...has done to your intended."

Ay-yay-yay. Mishegas. Craziness!

A round of feminine assent sounded in grunts of approval. The five of them now stood, facing off, their expressions devoid of embarrassment. "Whatever she did or didn't do, vigilante justice is against Colorado law."

Celia Jones had the good sense to look away, finally shamed, but Mrs. Abbott stepped closer to jab a finger into his face.

Rocky pushed Felicity behind his back.

He snagged Mrs. Abbott's finger and held on. "This is absurd, *ladies*. Felicity is a nice person.

Unfailingly polite to Temperance."

One of them snorted.

He narrowed his eyes, his temper percolating. "You think illegitimacy is contagious?"

Jennifer, the quiet redhead who hardly ever spoke in Rocky's presence glared at him. "I'm disappointed in you, Mr. Gideon."

"That right?"

"Yes, sir. I am. Disappointed." She swallowed, the movement visible in her slender, white throat. "You call Miss Percival by her Christian name. Overly familiar, indecent, and I'm shocked you're not more protective of Temperance. Shame on you."

"The next time Temperance is lying in the dirt with a pack of she-wolves atop her, I promise I'll worry." He set his jaw. *Why* was he defending Felicity instead of Temperance?

Because he comprehended Felicity instantly, deeply?

Why couldn't he understand Temperance's take in all this?

He loved Temperance...didn't he?

Of course he loved Temperance! He only sympathized with a kindred spirit.

One by one, they all raised their chins, glaring at him.

Fine, let this pack of wolves think they'd cornered the market on disappointment.

At his back, Felicity stiffened. *Feh!*—he still held her arm in his grip. He let her go and she immediately moved to his side, facing Temperance's friends with confidence and certainty.

A sight to behold with *shmutz* dusting her cheeks and dress.

"Mrs. Abbott," Felicity said, as if he weren't there, "Miss Celia..." She scanned the women, holding her own. "Your loyalty and devotion to Miss Cartwright is commendable."

"You *will* be on today's train," Mrs. Abbott ordered.

"My father invited me to this town, Mrs. Abbott." Felicity stood her ground. "I'm staying."

Rocky couldn't help it. His admiration for her doubled.

Felicity took two long strides toward the boardinghouse before turning, assessing them all once more. "Good day, ladies. Mr. Gideon."

She might be done with the she-wolves, but he wasn't done with her. Rocky took Felicity by the upper arm, swept up Mars's reins, and left the battlefield.

Felicity kept up, allowing him to remove her, but her fury showed in her rapid breaths, the ever-readable expression on her beautiful face, and the fists she clenched.

Ah, so she *did* possess a fine temper. Good.

Around a corner and into the alleyway, Rocky dropped Mars's leads, knowing the well-trained mount would stay put. "What were you thinking?" he demanded, "engaging a pack—"

She gasped. "*They* attacked *me*."

"I saw." His heart pounded. "To gain the upper

hand in situations like that, you can't let them close a circle around you."

"I *know*."

"Don't let them get behind you. They'll scatter before they get into formation—and that pack mentality—"

"I'm well aware." The gray of her eyes was nearly blue in the shade of the building. Sparks of fury—indignation?—captured him and wouldn't let go.

"Next time, you might find yourself outnumbered ten to one, maybe more."

"There won't be a next time."

"That's right. Even if I have to lock you indoors or escort you everywhere you go. Where were you headed, alone?"

She wriggled to free herself from his grasp—when had he latched both fists around her upper arms? He loosened his hold but refused to let go. She needed to understand just how horribly wrong things could have turned had he not intervened.

"Everywhere I go, I go alone." She refused to back down. No doubt what enticed the women to attack in the first place. "I needed air."

"You're supposed to be in the best room Mrs. Ihnken has. She told me she'd move you to the corner room with two windows."

"You!" The sparks of temper in her eyes, now nearly midnight blue, bored into his. "You meddler! You strong-armed mean old Mrs. Ihnken."

He lifted one shoulder in a lazy shrug.

"I don't need your charity." The woman was glorious when angry.

"This isn't about money, Miss Felicity. Money, I have. Never even notice a few dollars gone to help a friend. It's not charity—it's human decency. Kindness."

She opened her mouth, evidently ready to let another volley fly.

"It's too hot in the attic and you know it."

She couldn't deny that. Her fury ebbed. "Did I ask for kindness?"

"No, and you didn't need to. You're a lady, and you deserve every modicum of respect."

With sudden awareness, he realized this firecracker of a woman stood so near, essentially in the circle of his arms. She'd tipped her face up to his, the better to yell at him. So near, the fragrance of her freshly washed hair teased his senses.

He thumbed a bit of *shmutz* from her cheek.

Her nostrils flared. Her eyes rounded.

And just like that, he knew she was every bit as affected.

Irresistible.

One little dip of his head, a *bissel* closer...

Their mouths pressed, motionless... Held.

Without conscious intent, the intimate touch became a kiss. Powerful. Demanding and hungry.

His heart nearly seized as she participated, wholly, kissing *him*.

The fist to his gut nearly knocked him on *his tuches*.

Sanity screamed at him to halt, to control himself. But it felt so darn good—so right, so—

She wrenched free, her chest heaving, her wild expression made him want another kiss. No, a *hundred* more.

But...he'd kissed Felicity as if he'd never wanted anyone more.

When he'd all but promised to wed Temperance.

He soundly berated himself. *Farshtinkener.* Rotten.

The horror of his impetuous actions chased away the lingering glow. Dozens of sermons by the departed minister swamped his consciousness, reminding him of his duties, his obligations, how a gentleman *must* control his passions. The preacher had known all about the dangers inherent in giving in to desire.

How had he lost himself in the craziness?

He'd just kissed *his future sister-in-law.*

Chapter Nine

"Young men, watch yourselves that your kisses are chaste and carefully restricted. Kisses are promises and not to be given lightly. Many a fine marriage has been made when the first kiss is at the altar."
~ *The Gentleman's Guide to Courtship and Marriage*

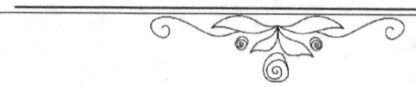

AGITATED FROM the fight with Temperance's cohorts, Felicity nearly vibrated. Rocky's dime novel hero routine had her thinking things she shouldn't. He'd merely intervened like a decent citizen. It hadn't meant anything more—

Until he'd kissed her.

At least she thought—*she hoped*—he'd started

it.

Shame flooded her overheated body.

She'd discovered, by age four or five, she wasn't allowed to play with other children. By age ten, she'd determined to show everyone, by her own actions, that they'd falsely accused her.

And what had she done?

The first time she'd been sorely tempted to toss self-preservation to the wind, she'd kissed the man who'd protected her—from a mean old woman and a bunch of do-gooders—and *liked* it.

Forbidden fruit.

The jumble of confusing, conflicting emotions battling in her head and in her heart was nothing more than an irrational craving for forbidden fruit.

Mortifying. She'd behaved wantonly, *ignited* a match to tinder as dry as the desert.

Thank goodness she'd put a stop to the insanity before anyone witnessed that kiss.

Ignoring everyone else out and about, she strode directly for Temperance Cartwright's door. *Alone.* Rocky's demands she go nowhere alone were utter rubbish.

Temperance had obviously started that whole incident. Felicity might have been ready to leave town, having learned as much as she'd believed she could, but after that incident—what had Rocky called it? The pack of she-wolves attacking?—Felicity couldn't allow Temperance the victory.

She'd say a choice thing or two to prissy Miss Temperance Cartwright. *Now*, before the other woman had the chance to hear of that kiss.

Rocky seemed like the kind of man to confess and beg forgiveness.

Upon reaching the Cartwright house, she opened the picket fence gate, strode straight up to the front porch and knocked.

No answer.

So Temperance was either out...or had seen Felicity coming, and knowing what her friends had been up to, opted to hide.

Rocky walked around from behind the house. *Must* the man run directly to his beloved to confess his sins?

He eyed her, his expression unreadable. "She's not home."

"I see."

"We need to talk."

"I do believe, Mr. Gideon, we've said all that needs saying."

Heat darkened his coffee-brown eyes. Memory of that volatile kiss paraded over his expression, plain as day. But no sign of regret...as if that kiss, to him, was anything but a mistake.

No way would she head down that path again. "That *never* should have happened."

He set his jaw, revealing anger and aggravation and...? What did she know about men's reactions to women they'd kissed?

"I won't repeat my parents' mistakes. I'm not that kind of woman, and I thought you knew that. Not a quarter hour ago, you defended me to those women."

He made his way closer in that loose-hipped rolling walk of his, shaking his head in denial. "That kiss was no mistake."

Her heart rolled over. He *couldn't* mean—He didn't actually think, after one kiss, one spectacular, toe-curling kiss—

The way he looked at her had the impact of a caress, or maybe a touch of his lips to her skin. "Stay."

Of all the things he could have said, that wasn't anywhere on her list. *Stay*? "Oh, you know I am. That pack of she-wolves, as you aptly called them, will not get the best of me." *I melted in your arms and kissed you.*

He stalked ever nearer, his boot heels thudding up three stairs to the porch. Near enough she caught the fragrance of his soap, horse, clean male, and sunshine. "You didn't cause that *mishegas*. You're too strong to turn tail and run."

"I'm *not* running." Not from Temperance's goons, anyhow. "I stayed long enough to learn all I can about Cartwright's motives. I've accomplished that goal."

His expression telegraphed he'd made his point. "You intend to catch tomorrow's train. Maybe the next day's."

"Why stay? There's nothing more to discover."

He shook his head and her traitorous heart leapt. "There is plenty more to discover."

She doubted he spoke of family history.

Memory of that kiss swept through her like a hot summer wind.

"Your father wanted you here." He'd lowered his voice. "Temperance wants you here. She just doesn't know it yet."

"My sister made her wishes clear."

His grin only heightened his appeal. Must the man have perfect white teeth?

"You just referred to Temperance as your sister."

"Did not." Oh, but she had. *My sister.* She'd never admit it, but she liked the sound.

"If you won't stay for your father, then stay for Temperance. Stay for your sister."

"I'll repeat: she doesn't want me here. The only thing I can do—" *for myself, for hope of a future with a man who'll love and respect me—* "...is move on." No sense spinning some tall tale about returning to St. Louis. "I'll be happier anywhere but Mountain Home."

He narrowed his eyes. He'd caught her choice of words. "Why are you here, on Temperance's porch?"

She edged up her chin. "I have a thing or two to say to her before I go." She'd ensure Temperance knew her shenanigans hadn't scared her. When she left town, it would be because she'd chosen to, not because her pack of wolves had chased her out.

"Do you, now?" She read realization in his eyes and the hard line of his jaw. He thought she meant that illicit, scorching kiss.

She wanted to set him straight. She also wanted

to let him stew.

"She'll be back, by and by," he said. "The back door is open. I suggest you wait inside. The walls of this place are thick and the interior remains cool. Besides, the place is half yours."

"Don't mind if I do." She brushed past him but he caught her and pulled her close.

"If you're worried I'm planning to tell Temperance about our kiss, don't fret. There's nothing to tell." She held his gaze, wanting to defend her vulnerability. "You kissed me in a fit of temper, not because you wanted to. It meant absolutely nothing."

Heat flared in his eyes, his pupils enlarged. "That's where you're wrong, Miss Felicity. I kissed you because I couldn't stand not to. I kissed you because I needed your lips beneath mine. Get on inside before I kiss you again."

ACCORDING to the clock on the kitchen wall, Felicity waited nearly an hour for her sister's return. Sitting at the table, she stared sightlessly through lacy curtains and mulled over the ridiculous things Rocky had said.

He'd wanted to kiss her...not once, but again?

He couldn't *possibly* have meant it.

The back door opened suddenly, catching her unaware. She pushed to her feet as Temperance entered the kitchen.

The time had come, and every prepared promise had evaporated.

She stared at her sister and her sister stared back.

Felicity found her tongue first. "We need to talk." No way could she admit Rocky—*Mr. Gideon*—had told her to wait inside. She must distance herself, refuse to think of him by anything other than the proper, formal address.

"I'm so glad you're here."

Wha—?

This was *not* the response she'd expected or deserved. *If she only knew.*

"I owe you an apology." Temperance untied her beautiful summer bonnet and set it on the table, then removed her gloves one at a time. She gathered both of Felicity's sun-browned hands in her pale, soft, white ones.

The contact, skin to skin, holding hands with this sister who was a complete stranger was disconcerting. *Odd.* Bizarre. And sort of wonderful.

She'd been prepared for battle, not an apology from a well-mannered Temperance.

"I'm ashamed," Temperance said, "for allowing my circle of friends to speak ill of you. They're good-hearted women, one and all. Protective. Generous to a fault. They'll love you once they know you. And they'll be ashamed they fought like schoolboys in the street."

"I won't be here long enough—"

"Hush now." Temperance's grip tightened. She sat and tugged Felicity down to her chair. "Can we be friends? Will you move in and allow us to become acquainted? I do believe it's what Father genuinely wanted."

"Why?" Of anything—*everything*—she should have, *could have* said in response, the one-word question echoed in the kitchen. After expecting tears and angry shouts, this abrupt about-face left her unbalanced.

What—or *who*—had changed Temperance's attitude?

"Why not?" Temperance's smile filled with sunshine and genuine warmth.

"Uh... because..." Because an hour ago, Felicity had kissed Temperance's intended. And that kiss hadn't been remotely platonic. And minutes before that, her gang had attacked.

"See?" Temperance's smile brightened further. "No excuses." With one last squeeze, she rose, went to the icebox and withdrew a pitcher of tea. She set the pitcher and two tall glasses on the table, followed by a crockery cookie jar.

"I paid Father's attorney another visit. I simply had to know, you understand, why Father would send for you now, not soon after my mother passed away. I can understand he'd withhold the information if only to spare her feelings. But she's been gone these six months. He had time."

Felicity craved the answer to that question herself. She accepted the glass her sister poured.

Whatever the attorney, W.W. Stuart, had told Temperance had utterly changed her stance, reversed her opinion, and if Felicity wasn't grossly mistaken, had genuinely opened the younger woman's heart to the possibility of a pleasant future. If not sisters, if not friends, then at least not enemies.

Temperance swallowed cold tea, considered a cookie dusted with confectioner's sugar but didn't reach for it. She swallowed and finally set her glass down. "My conversation with Mr. W.W. Stuart was most enlightening."

Felicity could have screamed with impatience. "And?"

"I always wanted a sister."

Felicity blinked, recalling Temperance's refusal to acknowledge her when she'd walked by the house. "And your conversation with Stuart?"

"I'm overflowing with happiness. And so soon after Papa's death, when I'd been all alone in the world, to have found you—for Father to have brought you to me—is the greatest gift I could have imagined."

Temperance sounded as if she saw this week's intolerable disaster as a bundle of sunshine and roses.

"I don't follow."

"You see, W.W. Stuart and our father—"

Our father. Had Temperance actually just referred to the old man as *theirs*?

"—met shortly after my mother passed away.

Father rewrote his will, instructed Mr. Stuart to locate you and bring you here for the reading."

Details she easily inferred based upon circumstances. It still didn't explain *why*.

"Mr. Stuart explained Father's feelings on the matter, his heartrending desire to make things right. You see, our father knew nothing of your existence until two years ago."

Felicity nodded, quite relieved Temperance had heard this from the attorney and not from her intended. That was one secret she knew Rocky—no!—*Mr.* Gideon—would rather not keep from his beloved nor be the one to tell her.

Amazing. The revelation seemed to have softened her sister's heart immeasurably.

"Mr. Stuart explained that Father loved my mother desperately. I'm sorry if that wounds you, my dear, but you did ask for the whole story."

Felicity nodded. She understood. Truly she did.

"It seems Father spent most of his life in penance for a youthful indiscretion—again, I apologize—and sincerely believed the only way to make amends was to keep his vow to wed my mother, for they'd been affianced a full year at that time. Father also believed, or so he confided in Mr. Stuart, the best he could do by your mother was allow her time and space and freedom to make her own peace with God and her conscience, and eventually wed someone far better than he."

What? Pious old goat.

Had her old man not once considered the

possibility of pregnancy?

Where was the lie? Had Cartwright loved Felicity's mother...or Temperance's? *Both*?

Did it matter?

She could comprehend throwing caution to the wind, for she'd done so herself, not an hour and one-quarter ago. But of all the irresponsible, ridiculous, absurd reasons—

"Felicity?" Temperance leaned in, showing more concern than Felicity could tolerate at the moment. "Are you quite well?"

No! She wanted to scream, to bolt out the door, to put more space between herself and this changeling who'd hated her yesterday, sicced bullies on her today, and now told tales she didn't want to hear.

She assessed the sister she didn't like and searched her *apparently* guileless face.

Had she concocted that absurd reasoning to make their father appear the dolt and wound Felicity?

Either Temperance was a mighty fine actress or she genuinely believed all that hogwash about God forgiving the repentant and making His sun to shine upon the penitent. Not her words, exactly, but definitely what she'd meant.

Never, not once in Felicity's life, had God heard *her* prayers for relief, though she'd tried for years and years to be the good girl, the obedient girl.

"Sister?" Temperance's cool fingertips on Felicity's chin shocked and provoked a flinch.

"What do you want from me?" The demand came out a bit too harsh, but Temperance was either quick to forgive or expected the barb.

Maybe both.

"All I want is for you to do as our father asked. I want you to move into this house. I want us to become acquainted, to try and be friends."

When something seems too good to be true, it usually is. "And?"

"I want you to meet the requirements of Father's will. You'll inherit this house and the money he set aside for you upon my marriage...to, um...Mr. Gideon."

All animosity had completely faded from Temperance's demeanor since these stipulations were read in W.W. Stuart's office.

Which girl was the real Miss Temperance Cartwright? The aggravated, frustrated, protective lady who couldn't bear learning her father hadn't been a saint...or the woman who welcomed a stranger into her home and offered to share her wealth, simply because Cartwright had loved her mother best?

"Please," Temperance whispered, "I have so very much. I knew Father. I'd like to share memories, photographs, stories of him. I want to accept his last gift to me...a surviving sibling. I *need* family, Felicity. I've been so horribly lonely since Mother died, and a tearful wreck since Father passed. I miss my brothers. I'm so *alone*."

Felicity knew the feeling. Mother had been her only family. Loneliness ached, a constant companion.

This might not be the wisest thing she'd ever done, but at the moment, she believed Temperance's sincerity.

"You know I've lost four brothers?"

Uh, no.

"You saw the twins' gravestone?"

"Yes."

"I'll tell you all about them all. Please stay. Please give us a chance—Father and me—to make you part of our family."

Seconds passed. Felicity squirmed.

How could she possibly convey the jumble of confusion and uncertainty and hope in her heart?

Temperance's sky-blue gaze seemed to brim with hope, mirroring Felicity's unspoken emotion.

"O.K. I'll stay."

Chapter Ten

"Young men, you will do well to seek advice from fathers, uncles, and mentors. Seek counsel from men whose marriages show every sign of happiness and success."

~ *The Gentleman's Guide to Courtship and Marriage*

"YOU'RE IN a fix." Mikkel Herschstein removed his eyeglasses and rubbed the bridge of his nose. He gazed over the porch railing at the large ranch he owned and operated.

In the near distance, Mick's beloved wife Ana weeded the kitchen garden that had shrunk in size since Rocky had lived here as a boy. Those five years had turned his life from hunger and desperation to abundance and hope.

Mameh, Tateh. Mama, Papa.

Both had more white in their hair than when last Rocky had visited. He needed to return more often. He owed his Jewish surrogate parents *everything*.

Rocky fought the urge to slink off Mick's spacious back porch, his tail between his legs. Quite a fix all right. He leaned forward, elbows propped on knees, and forced himself to meet *Tateh's* eyes.

Mick had taught Rocky a thing or two, most importantly how to live honorably. Other valuable lessons like hard work, confidence, self-assurance, and book learning. Mick's marriage was one of the happiest unions Rocky had witnessed, so asking his advice made a world of sense.

Rocky had confessed kissing Felicity Percival yesterday. And the riot of conflicting emotions keeping him awake at night.

Compassion in the old man's gaze piled the guilt in Rocky's chest higher and deeper.

He was stronger, *better* than this. He detested the loss of control, the selfishness he'd manifested in that alleyway and on the Cartwright front porch— *why* had he told Felicity he'd wanted to kiss her and would do it again?

Why, when his mother's selfish nature had destroyed their family?

Out of selfishness, he'd asked Felicity to stay...and she had.

She'd moved into Cartwright House with Temperance.

That was good. Good for Temperance. Good for Felicity.

Rotten luck for him.

Mick replaced his eyeglasses and stroked his long beard for thoughtful moments. "You've chosen your love, *zun*." Son. "Love your choice."

Rocky nodded, though not what he wanted to hear. "*Yo, Tateh*." Yes, Papa.

"You chose mighty well in the minister's daughter." Mick chuckled a little, easing the tension. "For a *skikse*, but we won't hold her Christianity against her."

Rocky tried to smile. What a pickle, given the minister's *other* daughter lit his fire in a way Temperance never had.

He'd wondered, a time or two, if Ma had left for another man. He had no memory either way. Could be she'd died. Maybe went home, somewhere back East. He might never know.

"You're right. Temperance is a wonderful lady." Until Felicity, Temperance had seemed the perfect woman for him.

"Yes."

Now he wasn't so sure. "What if I've made a mistake?"

"*Oy vey*. Every man wonders that, somewhere along the way."

"I'm not married yet. Am I doing the wrong thing by staying with Temperance?"

"*Hak nit in kop.*" Don't try my patience—but Mick had spoken with love. "Courtship is a promise. Courtship leads to marriage, and you two have been keeping company with that end in mind for more than a year, *yo*? Thirteen months? Fourteen? You came for my advice, I will give it."

Rocky nodded. He'd always trusted Mikkel's judgment, and he'd trust him in this most critical decision.

"It is time to propose. Put a ring on Temperance's finger. *Fershtay*?" Do you understand?

Bitter advice. Expected advice. "*Yo, Tateh.*"

"You've known Miss Temperance since age sixteen." Twelve years. "You watched her grow, knew her parents. You loved her parents."

All this was undeniably true.

"You just met Miss Percival. She's an unknown, an enigma. I'd hate to see you discard a diamond of the first water to discover you've chosen a lump of coal."

Mick was right, of course.

Temperance was a known quantity, and he felt genuine, abiding affection for her—if tepid.

He might, one day, love her with all his heart. He might, God willing, develop the kind of deep and immovable love Mr. and Mrs. Herschstein enjoyed.

It took *chutzpah* to let his attentions wander like he had—most uncomplimentary.

To leave Temperance now, with her father so fresh in the grave, was selfish. Far too selfish...which only evoked memories of Ma's abandonment.

He wasn't one to abandon a woman.

He'd prove himself a man that stuck. He'd make his vows and keep them. Their family would last through the decades, grow stronger with time, ensure safety and protection for their children.

Security and family were all he'd ever wanted.

He just had to remind himself that he wanted all that—with Temperance.

"I'll do it. I'll buy a ring and make it official."

"*Zei mit mazel.*" Good luck. "That's my good boy. You make me proud, *zun.*"

ON MONDAY morning, Felicity sat beside her sister on the sofa in the Cartwright family parlor, looking through photographs stored in an old hat box.

She held a photograph of Cedric Cartwright. Young, handsome and posing with a Bible.

"This was Father's ordination day." The man's expression radiated joy.

Felicity had spent three nights under Cedric Cartwright's roof. She and Temperance had stayed up talking, sharing stories, family heirlooms, books, pictures...and slowly, Felicity felt she'd come to know her father and his wife. She found she genuinely wanted to know everything she could about her heritage and the man she'd begun to think of as

Father.

Sunday services had been canceled as no replacement minister had yet been found. The sisters had stayed in and Temperance had shared tale after tale of Father's ministries to the people of Mountain Home and surrounding areas.

One picture at a time, one story at a time, it became harder and harder to believe Cedric Cartwright had been the seducer or evil-hearted man she'd always believed.

"Ooooh." Temperance leaning in, her shoulder brushing Felicity's. "Look at this one. It's the only photograph we have of my twin brothers and me together."

Temperance, blonde and solemn, sat on a bench with one adorable toddler on either side. Both boys wore short pants and frilly blouses, their pale hair severely parted. Identical, chubby cheeks and all.

She must have slipped into the past, her gaze clouded and distant.

"You miss them."

"Yes. Mother took their loss particularly hard. They were born minutes apart and when eleven years old, died within hours of one another, one late one evening and the other shortly before dawn." She drew a deep breath, let it out as if regrouping and smiled too brightly to fool Felicity. "It was a dark time. Four sons, and each one lost. I didn't think Mother would recover."

"Tell me about the other two."

"Mother's first was stillborn." Temperance

looked through the photographs. "Here it is."

Father, mother, babe in a long white dress. The infant appeared to be sleeping.

"They named him Adam Dumore Cartwright. Father's middle name was Adams after his mother's family and Dunmore was Mother's maiden name."

In the photograph, both Father and Annelise radiated sadness and a vacancy about the eyes. "When was he born?"

"December 17, 1855." Almost one year to the day Father had married Annelise. About eighteen months after Felicity's birth.

Temperance found another image slightly blurred by the baby's movement. Another long white dress and bonnet. "This is Neville Dunmore Cartwright. Named for Mother's father. He died just before his second birthday."

The child's pale eyes were open wide, his zest for life evident.

"He came third, after me." Temperance sighed. "Mother took Neville's death impossibly hard."

Comfortable silence filled the space as Temperance seemed lost in her thoughts and Felicity considered what it must have been like to experience siblings.

"Both of these brothers were born while we lived in Golden. They're buried there, side by side. Mother and Father took me and the twins to visit their graves once."

Felicity had wondered why all four boys weren't buried in the cemetery in Mountain Home but hadn't been willing to ask. "You're a good daughter."

"I took the *honour thy father and thy mother* lessons to heart."

Bonding with her sister was both glorious...and uncomfortable. Most of the misery stemmed from guilt. She'd *kissed* the man her sister loved. Temperance was open, giving, shared selflessly. Felicity, by comparison, had the darker traits. Distrust, doubt, theft. She'd stolen a kiss that should have been her sister's.

"I see you as a most obedient daughter." Felicity put the photographs they'd viewed back in the hatbox and selected two more. "I'm certain you were a good girl."

Felicity's heart squeezed, remembering the angst she'd put Mother through, including thousands of questions. "I tried. My mother didn't have an easy life. I didn't want to contribute to her unhappiness."

"See? Just what I meant." Temperance's expression clouded. Brooding, like a summer thunderstorm over the Rockies.

"What's wrong?"

"I feel so guilty," Temperance offered, her voice small and her emotion obvious. "Father made his wishes known through his will and I—"

Felicity took her sister's hand, squeezed.

"I disobeyed him." Temperance's throat closed, strangling her words. "I pray he wasn't watching from Heaven."

Felicity didn't know how much anybody could see once dead, or if they saw at all. But she understood guilt. "I know Father loved you. I'm certain he knew this would be a difficult time of adjustment. He had to have foreseen that much."

"You're too kind." She blinked, focused on two more recent cabinet cards, both photographs perhaps three by four inches each. She offered one. "This was taken two years ago."

Felicity took the card, peered at the older man, age lines bringing distinction to his features and gray hair pale about his temples. His face had filled out, his shoulders appeared broader. He wore a handsome suit of clothes, dark, with a white clerical collar. He'd been several months shy of his fifty-fifth birthday at his death.

She'd already asked so many questions over the past few days. What was he like? Did he have a lovely singing voice? What did he do when he wasn't ministering? Which chair was his? What did your mother call him? Who were his friends? How did he fill leisure time?

"What happened to him?" She hadn't thought to ask why Cedric Cartwright had died. Now, she needed to know.

"The doctor said his heart gave out. He'd been weak, sickly. He fought a lingering cough for years before he died."

Temperance choked up, and Felicity let her sister turn attention to the second photograph, taken before the same backdrop. Felicity's mother, Annelise, in an old-fashioned, bell-skirted woolen dress, buttons marching up the bodice's center front.

Her pale hair showed little gray. Her figure, fuller than in her youth, was still handsome.

"Your mother was a beautiful woman."

"Thank you. Tell me about your mother. What is she like?"

Not an easy question, but only because Mother had always been reticent to share details or information. "Very private. She didn't speak of her personal thoughts or feelings. A hard worker. She raised me on a farm near St. Louis that's been in Mother's family for generations."

"She's gone?"

"Yes. Cancer." Not one photograph of her mother had been taken, not at any time during her life. Poverty hadn't allowed for luxuries.

"When?" Temperance's gentle touch settled on Felicity's knee.

"Two years ago."

"Thank you for telling me about her."

Felicity nodded, at once missing her quiet mother and grateful for a new connection with her sister.

Temperance tucked those last two photographs into the hatbox. She closed the lid and looked up. "You must come with me this afternoon to the planning meeting for the Founders' Day celebration."

"Oh, I don't think I will." Mere days ago, she'd been attacked by Temperance's friends. No way did she want to sit through a planning meeting with them.

"I insist. It's a very good idea. They'll come

around when they see you and I are friends."

"Maybe."

"No maybe about it. Until then, I have just the thing for you." Temperance reached high on the bookcase built into the parlor wall between windows, and withdrew two leather-bound volumes, then two more. "This whole row of books," she indicated with a tip of her head, "are Father's journals. I'd like for you to read them." She passed the four books to her. "These are the most recent. I read them after the surprises in Mr. Stuart's office and found them most enlightening."

"Thank you." The trust in Temperance's actions humbled Felicity...and stoked her guilt. She really ought to tell her sister about *the kiss*. "I'm honored— and grateful. Thank you." Reading his words would bring so much more of Father's personality and innermost thoughts into focus. She imagined coming to know him through his written words. "Are you sure he'd want me to read these? They're so personal...and we never met."

"They're as much yours as they are mine. The volumes on the far left of that shelf are his earliest journals. Perhaps you'll find references to your mother."

No malice, no hint of spite, no judgment. It seemed this kind-hearted woman was the real Temperance Cartwright.

And perhaps, in the volume from two summers ago, she'd find an entry or two that shed light on Mother's letter. Maybe that entry would tell her more than Rocky had known.

"I hope you find what you need in here," Temperance told her. "I know all you want is answers. Your comments that night in Stuart's office told me so, and I just want you to know, dearest sister, if there is anything at all I can help you discover, especially if it brings you peace, I'll do it."

"Thank you." Felicity couldn't help wrapping an arm about her sister and hugging her as close as the journals allowed.

"I'm confident Father would be inordinately pleased to know you're interested in him." Temperance pulled away. "This book is one Father wrote a few years ago." She delivered a leather bound volume, twice as thick as his journals. "You'll like it. It's mostly a compilation of his thoughts on marriage, courtship, and the duty of young men in regard to both. He'd counseled plenty of young people anticipating marriage, and when he compiled the sermons and essays, he published it. That's where your inheritance came from."

How did Temperance know this? When she'd been unaware, until one week ago, that she'd had a sister?

Temperance chuckled. "The moment I heard the dollar amount in your bank account, I knew. Mother told me how much Father's royalty payments had been. We've always been comfortable and our needs were simple. Father set the money aside, in case of future need. But now I see, once he knew about you, he decided the money should be yours."

Felicity let out a breath. What irony! Her father authored and sold books detailing a young man's duty and moral obligations, when he'd failed in his obligations to her. The fact that he'd set aside the money he'd earned, chosen to give it to her, softened her heart a bit.

"But our inheritance amounts are identical. The will said your inheritance was the sum of your mother's inheritance."

"The rest of Mother's money is in the household account." Temperance smiled brightly. "We have an hour until it's time to dress for the planning meeting. Why don't you rest in your bedroom? I'm going to choose a pretty gown for you to wear to the meeting."

She'd never been one to accept charity. "I'm quite comfortable in this dress, thank you."

"Please, Felicity. I've never had the joy of sharing with a sister before. Don't spoil my fun."

Sharing was fun...everything but a man's affections.

The thought of Rocky—*again*—wrenched her heart and left her aching.

She clutched the books to her chest and nodded because the lump in her throat had lodged too tightly to speak.

She'd read and savor her father's words. And she'd give her sister the simple pleasure of sharing a dress.

Chapter Eleven

"The natural culmination of courtship is engagement and marriage. A properly courted lady will be as deeply in love with you as you are with her. You need not fear rejection for she will happily anticipate the moment you ask her to accept you as her husband."
~ *The Gentleman's Guide to Courtship and Marriage*

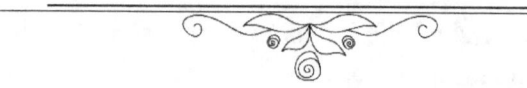

FIFTEEN minutes later, Felicity sat in the room her sister had given her...the bedchamber that had belonged to their father. Felicity could imagine Cedric Cartwright in this room, perhaps writing his book at the desk.

The two-story frame house had four bedrooms,

one in each corner. Father's, Annelise's, Temperance's, and the twins'. Felicity had seen Temperance's discomfort in disturbing her brothers' room, and no way would she be comfortable in Annelise's bed. Of the three vacant rooms, Father's had been her first choice.

Seated in the upholstered chair by the window, she thumbed through the most recent journal then through the typeset book Cedric Cartwright had written. *The Gentleman's Guide to Courtship and Marriage.*

She noted chapters on the subjects on courtship, selection of a spouse, admonishments on conduct, ensuring happiness in marriage, and more.

A word caught her eye: *seduction*.

Had it only been one week earlier that she'd arrived in Mountain Home, vehement Cedric Cartwright was guilty of seducing her innocent mother? She hoped to clear up the story by carefully reading his journals.

She read the section about seduction with care:

"I cannot say it any better than the esteemed Dr. Fowler from which I quote, regarding his condemnation of the crime of seduction (from Fowler's *Sexual Science,* 1870):

'...Think how pure and happy she was, and would have always remained and rendered those around her, but how inexpressibly miserable you have rendered her; all her former friends disown her; her strong social nature yearns for society only to be tortured by all her old associates taunting, instead of loving her; all worth knowing discard her; you have made her a lonely outcast.'"

Felicity sat motionless, allowing the poignant, outspoken passage to resonate in her heart and mind.

Dr. Fowler's statement had described Mother's circumstances perfectly.

It seemed The Reverend Cedric Cartwright not only grasped the enormity of what he'd done, but he comprehended the consequences to Beth Percival, Felicity's mother.

Rocky's retelling of the tears the preacher had shed upon learning of Felicity, twenty-three years after her birth, made so much more sense when cast in the light of these paragraphs.

Had Father written these passages with remembrance and regret? Had he hoped Mother had escaped such consequences, had kept their indiscretion a secret and moved on with her life, untouched by condemnation?

Was that why he'd wept upon learning of Felicity's birth?

The man who'd written these passages would fully comprehend his culpability.

She flipped to the front, seeking a publication date. *1876.* At minimum six months prior to the summery day he'd learned of her existence. Perhaps as much as eighteen months.

He'd already come to these conclusions before he'd learned about Felicity.

She pondered further, and in the quiet moments of reflection, she found it easy to let go of the harsh image she'd constructed of her father. He had cared. He'd comprehended the wrong he'd done them. In the end, he'd risked his legacy and reputation to try and make things as right as he could for his illegitimate daughter.

As if a two hundred-pound boulder were removed from her back, she felt remarkably free.

"FRIENDS, may I introduce Miss Felicity Cartwright." Temperance's arm, linked through Felicity's, tightened. "My sister."

Felicity froze. Yes, their father had asked that she bear the Cartwright name, but she'd not once thought of herself as Felicity *Cartwright*. Not even when she'd seen her reflection, finely attired in one of Temperance's best gowns, gloves, bonnet, and matching button-up shoes.

The shocked faces of the well-dressed ladies, taking tea in the parlor of a fine home, seemed stunned into silence.

One of them dropped a teaspoon upon thick carpet.

Just moments ago, they'd been chatting away, laughing, enjoying the intimate society of trusted friends.

Felicity forced a smile, though she met their

gazes head on—the same as she had four days earlier when they'd tried to *persuade* her to leave town. "Good afternoon, ladies."

Whether they accepted her or not, she and Temperance had accomplished their purpose, establishing unity.

"Good afternoon," Celia murmured, her golden curls a bit too perfectly arranged—at least compared to last Thursday when her coiffure had been spoiled by the tussle. She rose, and for a frightful moment, Felicity thought the woman might point at the doorway and order her out of the house. The scratch on the woman's cheek had faded. "I am Celia Jones. Welcome to my home, Miss Cartwright. Won't you join us?"

Quickly, the rest of the ladies followed suit.

Surreal, the experience of joining a circle of friends at tea. A first.

Tea was poured, a plate of little sandwiches passed, and within five minutes, the conversation flowed naturally.

Talk turned easily enough to the upcoming celebration, and the group asked Felicity's thoughts, preferences, and ideas.

Never, not once, in her twenty-five years had she been included in her hometown's Independence Day celebrations, church picnics, or the like. Out of necessity—out of habit—she'd lived on the fringes.

To be involved in the planning and preparations gave her a heady sense of inclusion.

"You must bring a luncheon basket for the

raffle, Miss Cartwright," their hostess insisted, her eyes bright and her cheeks pinked from the excitement. "You simply must."

The thought that someone would actually bid on, buy Felicity's picnic hamper, sit with her *intentionally*—set a competing race of tingles and chills along her spine. "Oh, I don't know—"

"Yes!" Temperance agreed with excitement. "You must. We'll cook together that morning, prepare our baskets. It'll be such fun."

With the hearty endorsement from Temperance Cartwright's seven closest friends, Felicity experienced a miracle unfold.

Maybe, just maybe, these women, with Temperance's lead, had the capacity to overlook Felicity's circumstances. And see her fully welcomed into Mountain Home's society, such as it was.

Or maybe the miracle occurred, more accurately, within herself. Perhaps she'd compounded the negativity she'd encountered...and excluded herself.

Temperance may have loaned her a pretty summertime dress of lavender cotton, but she'd inadvertently wrought an even more significant change within Felicity's heart and given her confidence, no matter where she eventually settled, she'd one day make genuine friends.

Warmth effused Felicity from fingertip to scalp to toe as she smiled at the eight women surrounding her in the Jones family parlor.

So, this is friendship.

Chapter Twelve

"More than one young lady, properly attended in courtship may at first decline your proposal of marriage. Take heart. She may yet accept you. Until she replies with a firm refusal, all is not lost."
~ *The Gentleman's Guide to Courtship and Marriage*

From the Journal of Cedric Adams Cartwright
Monday, August 29, 1853
St. Louis, Missouri

I HAVE fallen.
In love. Into sin. Into despair.

Would that I could recall the sands of time, watch myself, resist sweet kisses and carnal urgency. Would that I'd never followed her along the banks of the creek on her father's land. Would that I'd resisted the offer of my beloved.

I love Beth Percival more than my own life yet she has sent me away. Since that hot August afternoon when we yielded to temptation, she has shunned me. Today, she ordered me to leave, to return home. My employment will end in a few short weeks.

I fear I will never see her again.

I fear I have forever alienated my one great love.

I fear the sight of my face magnifies her guilt. I can do nothing to ease her sorrow.

I do not blame Beth for my weakness. The responsibility of this sin is mine and mine alone; I beg forgiveness of God, and of my beloved Beth.

I begged Beth to wed me, to make right our anticipation of marriage vows, yet she would not. I would have explained to Annelise; she would have understood. Our coming marriage is not a love match.

I do not comprehend Beth. She loves me, I know it. She knows my love for her is pure, complete, and I would wed her gladly and with rejoicing.

Would she have accepted me, wed me, had I not succumbed to temptation?

I am not the man she believed me to be.

I am not the man I believed myself to be.

What can I do but honor her wishes? She deserves so much better than I.

Dear God! Forgive me!

From the Journal of Cedric Adams Cartwright
Wednesday, May 22, 1877
Mountain Home, Colorado

TODAY, *word came from Beth Percival, my beloved, never forgotten.*

I grieve, my whole being anguished over the consequences of my actions, now nearly twenty-four years hence.

I have a daughter! Beth bore my child.

Beth's letter revealed little, only my daughter's name: Felicity Percival. She is well and living in St. Louis. My heart aches; I have missed the entirety of her life. I know her not. From all Beth did not reveal, I suspect our daughter knows nothing of me.

Percival is Beth's surname. Felicity bears her mother's name and not mine; I pray she did not suffer censure.

Oh, the pain of what might have been!

Why did Beth send me away?

I suspect Beth knew she had conceived and sought to test me. In my anguish, I foolishly obeyed her command. I believed she wanted me to stay away. Had I returned, tried once more to win her hand, would she have seen my love as trustworthy, true, and genuine?

I shall never know.

Tonight I confided the news in my beloved wife. We share all things. Joys and sorrows of ministering, the births and deaths of our sons, our joy in Temperance's goodness. Annelise's compassion offered absolution I do not deserve. The happiness we have found in our union is so much greater than I deserve.

Annelise's condition worsens. She grows weaker. Our days together draw to a close; I suspect my own days are limited. My consumptive cough worsens and my heart is too poor to travel, or I would go to my daughter Felicity, and beg her forgiveness for all she must have suffered in absence of a father.

From the Journal of Cedric Adams Cartwright
Tuesday, March 18, 1879
Mountain Home, Colorado

IT IS DONE.

My last will and testament, in the law office of W.W. Stuart.

My fondest wish is for my daughters to meet, to acquaint themselves one with another, to develop a familial bond so that neither is alone in the world.

The letter I sent to Beth Percival, two summers ago, was returned unopened, informing me she was deceased. I grieved her loss, with Annelise at my side, her tears mingling with mine.

Now my Annelise rests, her soul with God. The depth of my sorrow accelerates my illness.

It is best W.W. Stuart brings Felicity here, introduces her to Temperance. I haven't the strength or the heart. How could I bear the censure of either beloved daughter?

NEARLY FOUR weeks after her arrival in Mountain Home, Felicity had settled into living at the Cartwright house.

That didn't mean she found chaperoning her little sister comfortable in the least.

Felicity returned the refreshment tray to the kitchen and stored the lemonade pitcher in the icebox. One by one, she placed the glasses on the table. She needed a few minutes away from the courting couple and sensed they wanted a few moments alone.

She'd thought she'd been prepared for the eventuality of Rocky's coming courting. She'd lectured herself long and hard about how she would react, respond, and reply. The result? Muscles strung tighter than a vain maiden's corset.

Serving as chaperone made her ache with bone-deep sadness. Like dying of thirst within inches of a fresh mountain spring.

Despite her intention of being the invisible but present chaperone, her book open on her lap, she'd seen far too much. Rocky had been admirably, wholly intent upon courting Temperance, as he should.

No matter that the last month had given her much of what she'd desperately wanted—a place to belong, friends, the companionship and love of a sister, knowledge of her father...living here, with her heart and head tied up in her sister's intended destroyed her.

She might have told her sister she'd stay, but now, forced to witness them together as a couple, courting and falling in love, that proved impossible.

Maybe, once the pair married and moved into the grand house she and Temperance watched taking shape, living here would become easier. Father had left financial support equivalent to what she'd earned in twelve-hour work days in a farmer's fields near St. Louis. Here, she enjoyed far more than a tiny, rented room in a boardinghouse. All she did was share housekeeping with her sister, enjoy Felicity's company, visit friends, and minister to the sick.

She should want to stay.

But she had feelings for Rocky. Could she bear to watch him build a life and family with the woman he loved?

The conversation and laughter in the parlor ceased.

Trying to be a good chaperone, Felicity strained to listen.

"Oh, dearest Rocky, you're not—"

"Shh. Let me say this." A moment passed, then two. "Temperance Cartwright, our courtship has endeared you to me, brought us near to one another, shown me what our future will be like."

"Oh, Rocky—"

"Shh, darling. Please. Proposing to the woman I've selected for my bride is hard enough to do well without interruptions."

"Oh. Sorry." Temperance's giggle revealed nerves, strain, and happiness.

Felicity's heart jumped into her throat. Her pulse raced. Now? Really, must she listen to the man she'd developed tender feelings for propose to her sister?

She pressed her hand tightly over her mouth. Visions of the heat in his brown eyes as he lowered his head to hers, touched his lips to her mouth and leaned into that kiss—

Her nerve endings surged to life simply remembering that one glorious, forbidden kiss.

Temperance whispered something Felicity couldn't quite hear, then, "Oh, my dearest Rocky. I'm forever fond of you, you know that, don't you?"

Felicity choked. She couldn't stand by, overhearing the lovers exchange words of affection. If she bolted, they'd hear her footsteps.

Every word, each declaration, every sentiment tore at her heart.

"I beg your understanding," Temperance said, her voice tremulous. "I'm just so overwhelmed, with having just found my sister and grieving for my father."

"You're doing fine, sweetheart. Just answer this question: will you do me the extraordinary honor of accepting my proposal? Will you consent to become my wife?"

Silence.

Felicity strained to hear, the morbid scene on the other side of the closed door too awful to ignore.

A strangled sound—a sob? "I'm overwrought by loss." Tears distorted Temperance's melodic, lovely voice. "By autumn, Rocky, by autumn, I'm sure I'll be ready."

What was *wrong* with Temperance that she hadn't leapt with joy, squealed with delight, exulted in the thrill that Mr. Gideon wanted her to be his?

Felicity would have said yes. Immediately.

Pain ripped through her chest.

She'd known better than to want what she couldn't have.

Chapter Thirteen

"Young men, do whatever you must to save yourself
from wedding a woman you cannot or do not love."
~ *The Gentleman's Guide to Courtship and Marriage*

ROCKY SET another nail and pounded it into the
support beam. This deep in the mine, temperatures
hovered between cold and freezing.

"Hold it still, would you?" Short tempered,
cranky, and downright irritable, he'd lost his
manners but couldn't make himself care.

"Trying, Boss." Johansen, the gang lead,
narrowed his eyes in the yellow lamplight, obviously
doubting the answers Rocky had given a few hours

earlier when he'd arrived at Peerless Mine and thrown himself into physical labor, desperate to evict his demons.

"*Something wrong, Boss?*" Johansen asked.

"*No.*"

"*You don't sling a pick anymore. It's obvious something's eating you alive.*"

He glared, silently daring Johansen to continue.

"*You'd tell me if we was in the financial mire, right, Gideon?*"

"*Johansen—*"

If only this were about money.

"*Somethin' come across the wires from Washington? Silver dropping?*"

No, silver's price wasn't going to drek. Rubbish.

A minute slipped by, then Johansen tried again. "*You'd say if something bad happened, right?*"

Sweat ran down his spine and thirst demanded relief. He swiped a gritty wrist over his forehead, trying to catch the rivulets before they burned his eyes.

"Fetch another. Hop to." He dug in the pouch about his hips, stuck two nails between his lips and shouldered the stout wooden support, wedging it tight against the cavern floor and beneath the beam above.

Felicity's laughter sparkled, dancing through his memory. He chased the music away with two fierce strokes of the hammer.

Manual labor was supposed to shove thoughts of her beyond reach. Wasn't working. Not today, not yesterday.

He couldn't sleep, had no appetite, and nothing he did freed him from craving Felicity's company. He'd just proposed to her sister. What was wrong with him?

"Johansen!" Rocky's bellow echoed off the tunnel walls, amplified in the confined space. In a temper, he threw his hammer. The tool slammed against the rough-hewn wall and clanked onto the iron rail.

His chest heaved.

He'd started this project with four men at hand, and one by one they'd scattered. Slipped away like his sanity.

Rocky swore, loudly, in English *and* Yiddish.

He kicked his hammer out of the way, ducked beneath a low beam, and barreled toward the entrance.

Rounding the bend, he finally saw daylight at the end of the tunnel. No sign of his gang leader hefting in more support beams. "Johansen! Did I say it's quitting time?"

A stout figure stood back-lit by late afternoon sun. Too short and broad to be Johansen.

Koch. The foreman Rocky had put in charge of day-to-day operations because no one messed with him.

"Johansen hiding behind your skirts?" Rocky

demanded of his foreman. "Run to tattle to mama, did he? Where's the rest of the crew?"

Koch rolled a toothpick from one side of his mouth to the other. His grizzled beard had been trimmed, making his face even rounder. But the venomous glare in the man's ice-blue eyes told Rocky he'd finally found a man willing to fight.

"You want to tell me," Koch said, low but with threat, "why you run fifteen good men off the job today?"

They'd *quit*?

"Only four."

"*Fifteen*." Koch spat into the weeds. "Don't have to work with you to hear the cantankerous yelling. You do realize, with that strike in Leadville, rovers ain't gonna stay unless you give them reason to."

"Get them back." But Koch's expression made it clear that wasn't going to happen. "Offer a bonus. Ten dollars per man." Rocky had money. He didn't have excess miners.

Koch rocked back on his heels as if he hadn't just received an order. From the man *who paid him. To run this mine.*

"You quitting too?" Steam built and threatened to spill out his ears.

"Maybe. Maybe not. Depends."

"Spit it out, Koch. What do you want? Double the king's ransom I already pay you?" Irritation vibrated and his mind played tricks on him again. The image of Felicity's disappointment threatened to eviscerate him where he stood. She'd had that expression on her face as he'd said goodnight and taken his leave.

Minutes after Temperance hadn't rejected *or* accepted his proposal of marriage.

As if the release valve on his temper finally, *finally* busted open, Rocky's shoulders rounded. He flexed his fists, stretched the muscles in his neck...

Koch spread his boots, flexed his knees, and threw a fist with lightning speed.

And with the force of a cave-in, the source of his hostility came into focus. He'd finally traced the gold upriver to the source. After six or seven hours' exhaustive labor, he'd found the cause of his turmoil.

Temperance.

He didn't want the girl.

Koch's fist slammed into Rocky's jawbone.

"Ow!" Rocky growled, touched his jaw with a fingertip, and glared. "You *hit* me?"

"You threw the first punch." Koch danced out of the way, dodging Rocky's upper cut.

"Did not." He ducked, barely escaping a clobber to the left ear.

"Throw a fist at me, I'll throw one back." Koch scuttled away, putting a safe distance between them. "I don't care if you're the boss. Spit it out. What's chewing your backside?"

He'd foolishly, *stupidly* asked the *wrong sister* to marry him.

Thank God she hadn't said yes. But she hadn't yet responded with an irrefutable no.

Which left him in limbo.

"Lady troubles." Rocky glared at Koch. "There! Happy now?" His jaw smarted, his heart ached, and he detested himself.

Koch tossed back his head and roared with laughter.

Rocky had heard enough. He turned his back on the foreman and headed straight for the corral and Mars.

How could he have brought this *tsuris*—plague of epic proportions—upon himself, *willingly*?

"Boss!" Koch shouted. "No wonder you have lady troubles, ornery as you are. Sweeten up, knock some sense into your attitude. And always say 'you're right, dear'."

"Shut up, Koch."

Another chorus of chuckles, this time, Koch had company. Magnificent! Who else had heard the foreman's stupid advice?

He clenched his jaw to hold back a rock slide of curses, clear, finally, on what he must do.

As soon as possible, in the honorable and *right* way, as gently as he could manage, he'd leave off courting Temperance.

"DID YOU overhear Rocky's proposal of marriage?"

At the kitchen sink, Felicity scrubbed a little too

long on a dinner plate. She'd thought of little else in the two days since Rocky's fateful courting visit. "I did."

"I know it's been coming, for a long while, now..." Temperance dried a drinking glass.

How could Felicity adore her sister and yet harbor fierce jealousy? "I'm sure he understands. You need time."

"I told him so but he wasn't happy."

Because he'd wanted an immediate *yes*.

Temperance finished drying a serving bowl and set it in the china cabinet dominating one dining room wall. Through the doorway, Felicity watched her sister's posture wilt, her hand resting on the shelf. "I've been confused, so intrigued, so...fascinated and I fear I'm falling in love."

Of course Temperance would fall in love with her beau. That was the natural order of things, the purpose of courtship. And Rocky was an easy man to love. Gentle, kind, attractive, honorable, generous.

Temperance glanced up. Was that embarrassment on her face? Because she'd been caught wool-gathering about her future husband?

Felicity doused a pot in sudsy water. If her sister witnessed regret, longing, and unrequited love surely visible on her face...their brand-new bond would be shattered. "Those emotions are natural."

"Maybe."

She scrubbed mashed potato from the pot's interior. "You don't think attraction for an appealing gentleman is normal?"

Guilt flashed in the younger woman's eyes, followed by tears. "It just seems so...so...salacious. So *wrong*."

Temperance continued muttering, going on and on about something or another.

Was *this* what became of ministers' children? Prudery? Refusal of natural affection? Guilt over romantic attraction?

Perhaps Felicity's childhood had been better, after all. "Forgive me, but *nothing* is wrong with falling in love with a man. Did Father say such things were indecent?"

Temperance nodded. "I'm just so...*tempted*. I want to do things I shouldn't. I caught myself walking by his office last Friday morning, frantic for a...a *glance*. I spent most of the day desperate for another few minutes in his company though he'd invited me in the day before and I'd already spent a full half-hour during his work day—it's *so* inappropriate! Father would be *mortified* if he knew, and Mother—I can imagine Mother's chastisement for unladylike behavior."

Tears ran down Temperance's cheeks and dripped onto her bodice. She hid her face in the dishtowel and wailed.

The long, mournful cry broke Felicity's heart. She stilled, her hands in the dishwater, her heart pounding.

She'd never seen her sister weep in their scant month together. She'd shed a tear or two, understandable in her grieving, but had remained composed. Controlled. Sensible.

Felicity wanted to understand her sister, she truly did. But the emotional devastation made no sense. So what if she flirted with her beau or sneaked a few moments together?

Felicity dried her hands and grasped Temperance's trembling shoulders. "I'll help you to bed."

"No!"

"Do you need a doctor? Or a hot toddy—"

Temperance sobbed, weighted with despair, grief and guilt. All so *unnecessary*.

Unless Temperance and her beau had anticipated their wedding vows.

It happened. Often enough. Perhaps, as a minister's daughter, Temperance feared damage to her reputation. Understandable, certainly. Even if the wedding had to be moved up, to occur quickly, folks tended to forgive young lovers who welcomed seven-month babies. *After* their marriage.

"I'll fetch Mr. Gideon—"

"No! I can't bear to see him." She drew in a shaking lungful of air before making a strangled sound—half cry, half moan—and *thunked* her forehead upon Felicity's shoulder.

She patted Temperance's back, whispered soothing nonsense.

"I know you're thinking about leaving town." Temperance sobbed harder. "I saw the way you glanced at the depot on our way out of Pettingill's. Don't you know I *need* you?"

"You'll be all right, sweetling."

"I won't, not if you go away. I need your help."

"I'll help you." Temperance had more friends than any one woman could possibly keep up with *and* Mr. Rocky Gideon, but was gratified by her sister's plea. "Tell me what I can do."

"I can't face the celebration and all those people and everyone's questions wondering why I'm with *him,* why I'm enjoying myself, why I'm so h-h-happy...when Father's been gone only a month."

Anticipating the interminably long day, chaperoning her little sister while Rocky lavished attention on Temperance...she'd rather suffer a bout of cholera.

"I desperately want stolen moments with him, but it's so unwise—" She'd worked herself into a paroxysm.

Ah, young love. And propriety. And a desire to do the right thing and stay out of the kind of trouble Mother had found when smitten with Cedric Cartwright. How could she fault Temperance for ensuring protection of a chaperone?

"Don't fret. I'll stay."

"Promise? I can't be alone with Mr. Gideon. It just wouldn't be advisable. It truly wouldn't be."

"I promise." For this sister, she could suffer through *one* day in Mr. Gideon's company, could she not?

Temperance clutched Felicity tight. "I just...I really need you to let me...oh, I don't know." Temperance's hysterics swelled. "My heart can't be dissuaded," she said on a sob, "I've been trying for six long months, since Mother's funeral, to...to...but I just can't! I've been in love with him for so long. *So* long."

"I know, sweetling. I know." It seemed the worst of it wasn't over yet. No sense shushing a girl who needed to cry. "Let it all out."

"Do you understand? You see how much I love him? I *can't* be happy without him."

She must have realized, since Rocky's proposal of marriage, that her love outweighed her need for more time. Temperance wanted Rocky Gideon—and she would have him.

Loyalty to her sister must take precedence to all else. Family first, forever, and always.

Chapter Fourteen

"One out of twenty or thirty courtships proves the couple ill-suited for matrimony. Never act in haste; if, after exhaustive introspection, you determine consummation of your marriage would rain calamity upon your heads, inform her plainly. She may threaten a breach of promise suit but hold fast. Take your chances in court."
~ *The Gentleman's Guide to Courtship and Marriage*

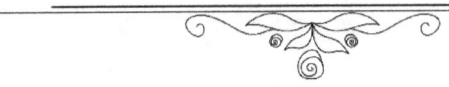

BETWEEN halting the defection of miners to the big strike in Leadville and rebuilding his reputation with his men, Rocky had done everything possible to intercept Temperance over the past two weeks. He'd needed a private moment to advise her of his change of heart, but failed.

She'd surrounded herself with her many friends, refused to see him, been away from home, or hadn't been where expected. Slippery woman!

Now that Founders' Day was upon them, unless he wanted to escort her about all day—which he most certainly did not—he had to ensure she gave him two minutes...and she *heard* him.

Obviously, Temperance was avoiding him. Likely because she'd not been ready to hear his proposal of marriage. The poor girl was evidently terrified he'd press his suit and urge her to answer in the affirmative.

With luck, she'd be happy to learn he would no longer court her.

At least he hoped so.

If he didn't soon corner Temperance, he'd have to wait until the raising of the flag had concluded. Poor timing for him to push through the crowd while everyone stood at attention, their hands over their hearts.

He caught sight of her wavy blond hair, tied back in a blue ribbon and headed after her—*again*. It seemed he'd chased her around the town green for the past five minutes.

Felicity had been at her side...until just now.

All the better. He'd rather avoid Felicity's disapproval as he terminated his courtship of her sister. Perhaps, if Felicity didn't witness the exchange, she'd be amenable to a future courtship herself.

Ah ha! His quarry stood at the edge of the crowd, half-hidden by a mature evergreen.

Rocky snagged Temperance's elbow.

She shrieked even as she whirled to face him. "Mr. Gideon."

"Good morning, Miss Temperance." He nodded at her father's attorney. "Mr. Stuart." The pair had been talking, their heads together.

He'd not seen Temperance this nervous, agitated, or upset since the reading of her father's will, and only then because of Felicity's surprise arrival.

But this cacophony of odd behavior also included...remorse? What had she been up to that evoked guilt?

Temperance gave up trying to slip from his grasp. "Please, Mr. Gideon, do unhand me."

Mr. Gideon? She'd called him Rocky as long as he recalled.

He released her, prepared to bolt after her if she ran. "A word in private, if you will."

"That's not possible." She faced him squarely, raised her chin in defiance.

"Miss Temperance," he said, "I'll be brief, and the topic is of utmost import—"

"Excuse the interruption, Mr. Gideon, but I only have a few seconds. I simply must explain myself before—" she glanced at the lawyer. "You see, I..."

He narrowed his eyes at the pair. "No, I don't see."

She sighed, a long, drawn-out breath that seemed overly dramatic. Instead of speaking, she turned to Stuart—as if he knew the workings of her mind.

Like the gentleman he tried hard to be, Rocky waited. She'd already spoken over him once, told him she could spare mere seconds. He motioned for her to continue.

"All right then. I'm very sorry, Mr. Gideon, but our courtship is over."

He raised a brow. Had he heard correctly?

"You mustn't fight me on this, sir. My mind is made up. I'm quite certain."

He wanted to laugh, to whoop with joy, to grab Temperance and swing her in a wide circle...he wanted to kiss her on the forehead.

He crinkled his brow, confounded. When was the last time he'd so much as *wanted* to kiss her...even on the brow?

"Well, *say* something. Just so I know you heard me."

He forced his face to relax. No smiling now. He couldn't laugh—that might hurt her feelings and earn him a clip to the jaw by W.W. Stuart who seemed to be in on the revelation.

"You've made up your mind," he repeated, splitting a glance between the pair, proving he'd listened.

"Indeed I have," she concluded. "Mr. Stuart and I are to be married. Today. We're eloping."

That caught Rocky by surprise. He split a glance

between W.W. and Temperance. So *that's* what she'd been up to. Her absences from home and usual social rounds. Her indifference to long periods between his courting visits. Her refusal of his marriage proposal.

He noted a familiar picnic hamper at W.W.'s feet. Not fifty feet away, on the street behind the park, W.W. Stuart's carriage and team waited. He'd caught the runaway couple just in time.

"I heard about your violence," W.W. said with exaggerated patience, "at Peerless the other day. I'll ask you to step away from my bride."

Rocky fought the urge to howl with laughter. Instead, "Does Felicity know of your intentions?"

Temperance's hackles rose. "Yes. We discussed it at length. She knows *precisely* what I intend. Well, perhaps not precisely, but she gave me her blessing. She understands love must find a way and true love is worth any cost. I know I'm disappointing Father and probably upsetting you, but you'll come to see, in time, this was the right decision."

He fought the bubbling happiness, pushed it down, and struggled to appear contrite. "I have no doubt you're right, Miss Cartwright."

"Goodbye, Mr. Gideon."

They two really did look well together. Both blond and refined of feature and a little on the silly side.

"Goodbye, Miss Cartwright. Mr. Stuart." He shook W.W.'s hand. "Congratulations. I wish you both every happiness."

"Thank you, sir. I must say, you're certainly

behaving as a gentleman."

"WE'LL OPEN the bid for Miss Felicity Cartwright's picnic basket. Do I hear two bits?"

When Felicity entered the basket auction, she'd somehow failed to comprehend that *she* would be on stage, the object of the bidding. Not the basket.

She—the spinster, illegitimate daughter of the preacher—had the attention of a crowd filling the town park and street. Dozens, no, *hundreds* of faces. Most of them strangers.

Miners, businessmen, ranchers. They all laughed, joked, and had a wonderful time.

She'd never felt so exposed. Her heart rate sprinted. This circus could easily make her the object of ridicule. She clutched the picnic blanket she'd brought along with her basket, twisting her fists into the fabric where onlookers couldn't see.

Where had Temperance gone? Felicity searched the crowd, desperate to find wavy blond hair, parted in the middle, a blue bonnet...

Why hadn't she insisted that her basket go up for sale *after* her sister's? Or simultaneously?

"Two dollars."

Every head spun toward the masculine voice Felicity would know anywhere.

Mr. Rocky Gideon, bidding on *her* basket. He'd ignored the opening request for two bits and inflated the price eightfold! Had he misheard?—thought Miss *Temperance* Cartwright's name had been announced?

Rocky's penetrating gaze never left Felicity's face. Embarrassed heat flushed into her cheeks. No. He wasn't mistaken at all.

Did he want to spoil her precious, new relationship with Temperance?

If he'd intended to spark interest in her basket, he'd gone too far. No one would challenge him for the ridiculously high water line of *two dollars*.

"I asked for two bits, Mr. Gideon," the gray-haired official called through his speaking trumpet, "but I'll take your two dollars."

A smattering of laughter from the audience. At least they were having a good time and weren't laughing *at* her.

Not yet.

"Who'll raise to two dollars, twenty-five cents?"

A man in a brown derby lifted his hand. "Two twenty-five."

"Do I hear two-fifty?"

Rocky climbed onto something—a chair, stump, or soap box—and now stood head and shoulders above the throng. "Five dollars."

Must her soon-to-be brother-in-law make a spectacle?

Sounds of appreciation melded with laughter and applause. Conversation buzzed.

Before the auctioneer could ask for another bid, Rocky cupped his hands about his mouth and yelled, "I raise to seven-fifty."

Good humor echoed in the growing enjoyment. A man she didn't recognize hollered, "Hey, Gideon, you know which Cartwright girl you're courting?"

Oh, no. No!

With sudden mortification, Felicity recalled her sister's tearful hysterics. Temperance intended to accept Rocky's proposal. She'd be so hurt, watching in horror as her beau bought her sister's basket *instead.*

Humiliation and shame heated her cheeks. She should have fled the moment the bidding started. The food didn't matter, nor did the dishes. It was all replaceable—but her precious little sister's heart was not.

"Indeed I do." Rocky's focus never strayed from Felicity. "I most certainly do."

She gasped, outraged. Rocky was most certainly not courting *her.*

Rocky courted Temperance. Had done so for more than a year. People knew that. They should be disappointed, shaking their heads, complaining. Not *enjoying* this.

Something was seriously amiss.

She glared at Rocky.

The man had the nerve to wink.

Her mouth opened in shock. What did he know that she didn't?

"Do I hear eight?"

Mr. Brown Derby signaled.

Rocky shouted, "Fifteen."

"Sixteen!" Derby returned.

Excitement surged through the crowd.

With her heart pounding double-time, she scanned the line of picnic hampers. Then searched a second time. Temperance's basket wasn't among them. Felicity had been beside the platform from the beginning. Temperance's turn had not come and gone.

Every head swiveled, awaiting Rocky's response. "Twenty."

"Twenty!" the auctioneer bellowed. "Going once!"

The crowd's murmurs swelled.

All heads swiveled toward Mr. Brown Derby who shook his head in comical defeat.

"Going twice."

"Fifty dollars." Rocky's announcement brought stunned gasps, punctuated by shrill whistles and hearty applause.

Felicity's heart lurched. Her head buzzed and vision grayed. *"Fifty. Dollars."*

"Now, Mr. Gideon." The auctioneer's jolly chuckle made Felicity cringe. "You do realize, Mr. Gideon, in all twenty years of Mountain Home's Founders' Day picnic basket auctions, the most anybody spent was six dollars, fifty cents. You trying to purchase that church organ all by yourself?"

A wave of chuckles rippled through the audience.

"Yes, sir." Rocky's grin widened, a dashing figure in his suit of clothes. The gold watch chain at his vest buttons and pocket winked in the sunlight. "The church organ is a fine reason to open my pocketbook, though the far *better* reason stands at your side. An even hundred dollars."

No, no, *no*!

The air seemed to vibrate with the wild applause, shouts, whistles, and claps on Rocky's back as he pushed through the crowd toward the platform.

Dizziness stole Felicity's balance. She might have swooned, if the announcer hadn't taken her elbow in his hand, somehow anchoring her.

Too late.

How had this happened?

"Make way for Mr. Gideon," the dignitary cried through his brass cone.

Rocky had already withdrawn paper currency from his wallet. He clutched the bills high over his head as the crowd parted, funneling him toward the stage. His boots thudded on the wooden steps of the platform.

He presented crisp twenty-dollar bills to the auctioneer, one at a time. The crowd counted along. "Twenty, forty, sixty, eighty," they chanted in unison. "*One hundred.*"

The dignitary offered Rocky a handshake. The men grasped hands, pounded one another on the back.

The townsfolk whistled, clapped, and cheered.

The auctioneer lifted his speaking trumpet and

yelled, "Sold! Miss Felicity Cartwright's luncheon basket, *sold* to Mr. Rocky Gideon, for *one hundred dollars!*"

Felicity closed her eyes as applause thundered like a locomotive chugging past at full speed.

Gradually the noise diminished. She opened her eyes to see Rocky holding the voice trumpet aloft, signaling for quiet. "In case any here haven't yet heard the joyful news, Miss Temperance Cartwright and W.W. Stuart eloped. I wish the bride and bridegroom every happiness."

What? Felicity—married? To W.W. Stuart?

She fought the urge to swoon.

"Hear me, gentlemen: *I* am courting Miss Felicity Cartwright."

Chapter Fifteen

"A proper courtship begins by presenting yourself as a suitor, with genuine intent, to win the hand of the lady you have selected. Await her acceptance of your suit. Progressing in this manner ensures your love and money are invested in one who fully intends to wed you."

~ The Gentleman's Guide to Courtship and Marriage

COURTING her, indeed!

Jumbled emotions fought for dominance. Humiliation. Surprise. Anger. Happiness.

Too much. Far too much.

She turned the corner onto Church street and

broke into a trot. Her heart pounded and her breaths quickened.

Home. She had to get home.

Rocky had called after her, followed, but she'd not acknowledged him. How could she? She didn't know if she'd attack or throw herself into his arms. Neither would be appropriate given every eye in the county looked on.

Tears filled her eyes. She would *not* cry.

Had everyone in town known of her sister's plans, everyone but her?

Perspiration trickled down her back as she refused to look up at a passing wagon, then cut across the street. She ran, her borrowed skirts tangling about her ankles. She grappled with the excess fabric, holding it up, praying she wouldn't trip.

Gravel grated beneath the boots of someone behind her. One quick glance—Rocky, the picnic blanket thrown over his shoulder and the basket in one hand.

He'd followed her all the way home.

He couldn't see her like this, unraveling at the seams, likely to sob has violently as Temperance had that Sunday night, two weeks before.

Flashes of memory only compounded her confusion. Temperance, woolgathering. Temperance's face, dripping with tears.

How, exactly, had she missed the significant clue that her sister spoke of someone other than Rocky Gideon?

She suspected she knew why—she, herself,

couldn't focus on anyone else. Rocky filled her thoughts and her heart so thoroughly, she couldn't comprehend Temperance could love anyone else.

And she detested him at the moment.

She dashed her sleeve across her eyes, cursing the unwelcome tears.

Finally at the back porch, she clomped up the stairs and turned the doorknob.

Rocky's free hand settled at her back.

She drew a shaking breath, fought for control, and squeezed her eyes shut. The yellow roses smelled too strong, too potent.

He shifted, evidently setting the basket and blanket down on the stoop. He must have turned to her or maybe she stepped into his arms. Either way, she found herself surrounded by him, her cheek pressed against the warmth of his suit coat.

His chest rose and fell in even rhythm. Despite her own breath scouring against her ears, she fancied she heard the steady beat of his heart. She should push away, should tell him to leave and take his absurdly expensive picnic with him. But his embrace felt so good. Just to be touched by him, held like this...

She pushed away.

He let her go. "I never meant to embarrass you."

Emotions tumbled, played tug-of-war. Frustration won. "What were you thinking?"

Regret etched his features. "I hoped you'd be happy to accept my suit. I should have asked you properly."

Apparently the man thought the only problem was his bold pronouncement, claiming her in front of God and everyone. She waved both hands to banish that thought. No way could she focus on that yet.

"Yes, you should have, but that's not the trouble here."

"It's not?"

"My sister eloped and *everyone* in this town knew but me?" She needed something to pin her frustration on. Confusion and concern in Rocky's eyes diffused her anger, at least toward him. The warmth of his hand seeped through her sleeve and felt so achingly good.

His brows drew together in confusion. "She said you talked about it and she had your blessing."

"No." Temperance's aggravation and tears had been about *Rocky,* not W.W. Stuart. She swayed, dizzy.

Rocky took her elbow and ushered her inside. He settled her in a kitchen chair, collected the picnic hamper and blanket, then shut the door against the sun's direct rays.

He worked the pump, filled a glass, and brought it to her. "Drink."

The water was cool and sweet but did little to drown the memories of Temperance's sobs and hysterics on that Sunday night, two weeks back. Much of it was jumbled, out of order, and surely not complete. Something about the town's judgment if she were too happy this soon after Father's passing. Refusal to see Rocky.

She held the glass against her temple and closed her eyes against the truth.

She'd utterly misunderstood her sister's pleas for help. "How did I let this happen?"

"Your sister's a grown woman."

"But *eloping*?"

"It's what she wanted." He pulled out a chair and sat beside her.

"So you bid obscenely high on my basket, to...what?" She groped for an answer. "Get back at her? Save face in front of your friends and neighbors?"

He chuckled softly, his expression relaxed and open and happy. "Any idea how long I've been trying to corner Temperance, determined to inform her my courtship was over?"

That couldn't be right. "You love Temperance. You proposed marriage. You're smarting because she didn't say yes."

"I thought I was doing the right thing, the best thing. I believed redoubling my focus on her would cure my burgeoning love for you. I was wrong."

L—love?

Tingles skipped along her nerves, raising the fine hairs on her arms. He fancied himself in love—with *her*? Some questions simply had to be asked. "Wrong?"

He nodded. "I was wrong to think marriage to Temperance could make me stop loving you."

Love.

Her heart leapt into her throat and lodged

there, beating far too fast. She made a noise of disbelief.

"You, my dear, understand *me*. My need for stability, for a woman who will stick. You and I are cut from the same bolt of cloth. Two people who need and want the same thing—a family to call our own. We value it more because of all we missed out on. We're stronger, together, for choosing to build that solid foundation, side by side."

He took her hand in his. "I bid on your basket with purpose. First, I was finally free to seek your company and wanted nothing more. I've spent two weeks trying to officially end things with your sister so I'd have a chance to win you. Second, I had to stake my claim before someone else stole you away."

"That's absurd." Her head spun. "No one is interested, Mr. Gideon. I've never been courted."

"Make no mistake, Miss Cartwright, I *am* courting you." He leaned near and pressed a kiss to her temple. "You're mine."

The intensity of his claim stunned. "One hundred dollars? Why not cease at twenty?"

He chuckled. "How many times do I have to tell you it's not about the money? I have money. I like the idea of the church finally buying an organ. I wanted every man, woman, and child to know you're mine."

She couldn't speak, couldn't think. Her world had flipped onto its side, wheels spinning ineffectually.

He took her hand between both of his, stroked his thumb over her knuckles. "I apologize for announcing myself to the whole town before speaking with you. But I'm asking now. Accept my suit. Say yes."

"I—" Parched, she wished she'd drunk more water when she'd had the chance. "I don't understand you."

"That day in my office, I felt a connection. I told you things I've never told a soul and you understood. You know my reasons for wanting to build a marriage that will last."

He'd spoken of Temperance then, not *her*.

"I adore you, Felicity Cartwright. You're with me constantly." He absently rubbed at his chest as if his heart ached, but quickly brought his hand back to hers as he couldn't resist touching her. "I admire your *chutzpah*, the way you held your ground with Temperance's she-wolves then stood up to me. I loved the way you kissed me back."

She fought a grin.

He leaned in slowly, announcing his intent to kiss her. He allowed several long moments. She could have refused him, turned away from his kiss, but she wanted it. *How* she wanted.

"I've remembered our kiss a thousand times," he whispered. "I kissed you because I couldn't stop myself. I've wanted your kiss, ached for it, every day since."

The touch of his lips to hers was magic and fireworks and a prayer. Warm, supple, sweet. He withdrew and traced a fingertip along her cheekbone. "I will convince you slowly, one day at a time, that you and I are wholly suited to matrimony."

The affection and earnestness in his expression made her insides tingle. "I'm new to this..."

"That's O.K. We have your father's help. He wrote a book of advice and counsel and important considerations. Everything I know about courtship I learned from him."

"I've read *The Gentleman's Guide to Courtship and Marriage*."

A wry grin tugged at his lips. "I'll admit, his advice is usually solid, but I took him too literally a time or two and landed in hot water."

She lowered her lashes, smiling.

"This courtship," he vowed, "will be fairytale worthy. I'll do things right this time." His lips touched her neck, little thrills erupting as he brushed the tender skin. "I meant what I said, Felicity. I'm wholly focused on you. This courtship will end in the happily wedded blissful state I've craved my entire adult life."

His confidence expanded, filling her with warmth and life and certainty she'd never known. It filled the voids and hollows and emptiness she'd lived with...well, forever.

He kissed her jaw then tugged gently on her earlobe. "I've mentioned love twice now, and you haven't panicked. That's good. I hope you remained calm because you already knew I'm in love. With you."

Her heart skipped—but not with panic. Pure joy. Amazing in its purity.

He eased back, held her gaze. "I'm determined to win your heart. And I will."

The depth of affection she witnessed in his eyes banished her objections. "You already have it."

Happiness illuminated his countenance. "So that's a yes? You accept my suit?"

Joy bubbled over, rich and growing and wildly exciting. How could she say no? "Yes."

He whooped with elation. He stole a kiss, then two.

"I'll try," he whispered into her ear, minutes later, "but I doubt I'll be able to give you a full year of courtship before I ask you to become my wife. When I do, I'm banking on you saying yes."

Chapter Sixteen

"Bear in mind the lady's inherent privilege to refuse your proposal. You will, in time, find another young lady deserving of your love and exult in the good fortune resulting from the first lady's rejection."
~ *The Gentleman's Guide to Courtship and Marriage*

Epilogue

IN THE SPRING of 1880, Mountain Home's river overflowed its banks with late spring snowmelt, and the view of said river from the new house Rocky had commissioned for his bride-to-be showed the vibrant green of new grasses and wildflowers.

A perfect backdrop for the question he'd determined to ask.

The timing couldn't be better. He'd shown her through the house, the final interior details completed over the winter. The spacious rooms smelled of sawdust, plaster, and paint. All it needed was a woman's touch. Details like furnishings, someone to set up housekeeping, and in time, the pit-a-pat of little feet.

Rocky walked hand in hand with Felicity—truly his one source of merriment, contentment, and delight. His lady's name suited her perfectly.

She suited *him* perfectly.

For not the first time, he thanked The Reverend Cartwright for bringing his bride-to-be into his life.

"I have something to ask you," he told Felicity once they reached the rushing river.

"Oh?" She turned to him, evidently still considering the house and all it meant.

"We've been courting for nine months."

"Five days shy of nine months." She smiled with heartwarming trust and affection and love.

Humbled, moved, he raised her hand and kissed her knuckles.

He held her gaze while he lowered himself to one knee. Moisture from the damp grass soaked through his pant leg but he didn't care. The brilliance of joy on his bride's face filled his heart to bursting. Tears spilled over her lids and trailed down her cheeks. Happy tears. Joyful tears. Love and acceptance and promises, all rolled into that beautiful expression.

"If I had more patience, I'd give you another four or five months, give you time to decide if I'm the best match for you but the truth of the matter is I can't wait another day."

She squeezed his hand between both of hers. As if too choked to speak she simply nodded.

"Will you, dearest Felicity, marry me?"

She nodded, vigorously, and threw herself into his arms. He caught her, held her tight, rocked her back and forth and savored every moment. The sunshine, warm on his shoulders seemed heaven-sent as if her father were aware and approved.

"Is that a yes?" He kissed her hair. "I need to hear your answer, my love."

She laughed, her cheek pressed to his shoulder. "Yes. Yes! I love you, Rocky."

He chuckled, joy as abundant and overflowing as the river.

He could see now, with perfect clarity, he and Temperance had never been a good match. He'd seen it nine months ago—probably much sooner—and nothing had changed. The gal had blossomed as Mrs. W.W. Stuart. She and the attorney were happy as two peas in a pod, had set up housekeeping in a nice house on the east side of town.

Even better, the sisterly relationship between Temperance and Felicity had deepened, strengthened, become what the minister must have hoped it would. The bond between them defined *family*: permanent, resilient, special.

Rocky gave his bride-to-be one more squeeze and held her away just enough to see into her eyes. "I love you, Felicity. I think I've loved you from the moment I saw you in W.W.'s office."

"Balderdash." But she'd found her voice and smiled through her happy tears. "You fell in love with me when you told me all about your parents, I denied your responsibility, and you discovered our similarities."

"You're probably right, my dear."

"Probably?"

He loved it when she teased. "My mistake, love. You're right. Of course."

He claimed her mouth, kissed her with the reverence she deserved. This precious woman owned his heart. "Happy birthday, love."

"Ouch. I'd rather not think about birthdays. I'm an old maid. Twenty-*six*."

"You're hardly old and you won't be a maiden much longer." He waggled his brows, anxious to put his wedding ring on her finger, anxious to claim her and address her as Mrs. Gideon.

"You're incorrigible."

"Nope. Just a man in love." He kissed her, a quick touch of lips. "Don't I get credit for remembering?"

"I suppose you do. But remember that my birthday, all of my life—until you, of course—was no cause for celebration. That day reminded my mother, and everyone else, about the circumstances."

"That's their problem, not yours. I'm glad you were born, and it's my opinion that matters."

"Thank you. Now let's talk about something else."

She hadn't made a move to extricate herself from his hold and he liked the way she fit against him. Just right. "Let's set a wedding date."

She stilled in his arms.

"Felicity, darling, no rush. I just thought, with summer coming, you might want—"

"Is it really up to me?"

"Of course it is. The bride always chooses."

"Then I choose today."

Speechless. She'd rendered him *speechless*.

"No comment?" she teased.

"Don't you want time to have a dress made? Mrs. Pettingill at the tailor shop sews exquisite—"

"No."

"But your sister—don't you want—?"

"You're handsome when flustered." This time she kissed him. With heat and enthusiasm and love.

"Don't you want time to make plans? Invite friends? I don't know—decorate our new house so we might be married there?"

"It took a crisis to bring us together, Mr. Gideon. I waited twenty-five long years to find you, and now that you've courted and wooed me, and finally proposed marriage, I don't want to wait one more day. I love you."

He nodded. She'd said everything that needed saying.

"Besides, if May fifteenth becomes our wedding anniversary, my birthday will become a day to cherish—the day we took our vows as husband and wife."

"You're most convincing."

"If it's good enough for my sister, it's good enough for me. Eloping will become a family tradition. Let's hurry into town, obtain a wedding license, and locate the new pastor."

"You're sure?" He knew he shouldn't ask. Why would he resist when she clearly wanted precisely what he did? Happily ever after couldn't commence soon enough.

"Yes, I'm sure I want a minister to officiate at our wedding." A twinkle illuminated her beautiful eyes. "In the church my father built. It'll be almost as if he were there."

"I think we'll find The Reverend Gilbert easily enough. Shall we swing by your sister's house and invite her to witness the event?"

"Yes, though I'm still put out she didn't invite me to attend her wedding. She left me behind."

That tugged a deep, hearty laugh from Rocky, one his bride quickly joined in.

"But darling," he teased, "you're so quick to forgive."

That brought a sweet smile to her face, one that seemed to light her from within. "It's you who taught me acceptance and forgiveness and the meaning of family, Rocky Gideon. And I can't wait for our life's adventure to begin."

"Ready?" He asked, twining his fingers with hers, tipping his head toward the waiting team and buggy.

"I'll race you!" She squealed with laughter, pulled free, and bolted for the conveyance.

ON MAY 15, 1880, Rocky Gideon and Felicity Cartwright were joined in holy matrimony by a very green, very young replacement minister of the gospel, in the church Felicity's father had built.

No one had ever accused Rocky of being quiet about good news. He shouted a few joyous announcements on their way through town, so it turned out half a dozen—or perhaps a couple dozen—bright-faced townsfolk joined them just in time to witness the joyful occasion.

Felicity's sister, heavy with child, entered the church, *schlepping* her attorney husband close behind. Temperance nearly called a halt to the services, exclaiming she had the right to witness the ceremony from beginning to end but Felicity's calm reminder that Temperance had eloped thus negating all requests her little sister might make.

Red faced, The Reverend Gilbert stuttered, coughed, backed up a phrase or two, but ultimately completed the ceremony. Rocky pushed a heavy gold band, mined from the Peerless, onto his bride's fourth finger and kissed it. The preacher pronounced them man and wife, then presented Mr. and Mrs. Rocky Gideon to the cheering onlookers.

A plump, white-haired matron pounded a few vigorous cords on the piano by way of recessional. The happy couple, dressed in simple every-day work clothes, jumped in their buggy, still standing at the church steps. The crowd waved them off with shouted well-wishes and applause.

The onlookers watched, perhaps with a bit too much attention as Rocky drove the buggy next door to the Cartwright house, scooped his bride up in his arms, and shouted to his brother-in-law to put up the horses.

With that, Rocky carried Felicity up the stairs, over the threshold, and into their very bright future.

~ *The End* ~

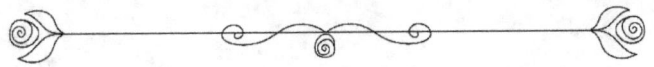

Please share this book with a friend.

It's easy to loan a paperback book.

Please recommend this book.

Please share your thoughts on this book
with friends.

Please post a review.

Reviews from readers make all the difference to those
browsing and buying, as well as to writers. Please
take a moment and leave an honest review—just a few
words will do.

www.kristinholt.com/review-
courting-miss-cartwright

and

on Goodreads.com
http://bit.ly/2czZQPC
(case sensitive)

Dear Reader,

Thank you for visiting 1879 Colorado with me. Mountain Home, Colorado is a fictional town in a very real place. I've built a series (*Holidays in Mountain Home*) set in this small town leading up to the turn of the century. When determining where this novella would be set, I chose Mountain Home and the residents and locations that would have been there in 1879. This novella is linked to the *Holidays in Mountain Home* Series without being a numbered volume in that series, because...

This title, Courting Miss Cartwright, is Book 2 in the *Six Brides for Six Gideons* series. Book 1 in this series is *Gideon's Secondhand Bride*. The hero in each book of this series are brothers, all with the surname Gideon. They became separated as children, and by the end of the series, we'll see if and how and when they reconnect.

So while this book is officially #2 in the *Six Brides for Six Gideons* Series, it's also a tie-in to *Holidays in Mountain Home*. What holiday falls within its pages? Founders' Day! I hope you enjoyed the small-town celebration commemorating the town's original settlement and the sense of community, belonging, and home.

More than one newcomer (character) has found the ever-elusive sense of *home* in Mountain Home,

Colorado. I hope you'll give *Maybe This Christmas*, *The Marshal's Surrender*, and *The Drifter's Proposal* a try.

A real book titled <u>*The Marriage Guide for Young Men: A Manual of Courtship and Marriage*</u> <u>by Reverend George W. Hudson</u>, was self-published in 1883 from Ellsworth, Maine (see the online resource at the close of my note). I enjoyed reading about the Victorian American attitudes regarding courtship and marriage, and the advice given to young men seeking to wed and do so with happy results.

This public domain book sparked my creative process in plotting this story, and while I do not quote the book, I drew upon the pervasive themes and belief system of the era to ensure historical accuracy for the quotes from my loosely based fictional Victorian self-help book.

This fictional book exists only in the quotations cited throughout this novella. The fictional 'book' is by my character, The Reverend Cedric Adams Cartwright and is titled: *The Gentleman's Guide to Courtship and Marriage*. This fictional publication required a date early enough to have guided Rocky Gideon's selection of a well-suited wife (and the mess that well-intentioned advice caused).

My inclusion of the Victorian-era quotes was not meant to poke fun but to add a layer of historical truth and better explain Rocky's motivations. I sincerely hope I succeeded.

My choice to include a valued Jewish character

and a smattering of Yiddish is in nod to my own heritage. While Jews were in the minority in the west (aren't we, everywhere?), pockets of Jewish communities existed historically in Denver, Phoenix, Salt Lake City, etc.

As always, I welcome your comments and thoughts. If you enjoyed this book, I'd greatly appreciate a review. Thanks in advance! You're also welcome to contact me through my website. I'd love to hear your thoughts on *Courting Miss Cartwright*.

Warmly,

Kristin

P.S. You'll find the true-to-history book by Reverend George W. Hudson online, *The Marriage Guide for Young Men: A Manual of Courtship and Marriage*.

See:
http://bit.ly/2cmNrfY
(case sensitive)

Books by Kristin Holt

www.KristinHolt.com

And while you're there, please sign up for her newsletter. *Be the first to hear about new releases, sales, and subscriber-only extras.*

Quick Peek: Amazon's Kristin Holt Page

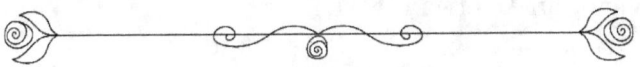

Learn more about Kristin Holt's Series:

THE HUSBAND-MAKER TRILOGY

PROSPERITY'S MAIL ORDER BRIDES

SIX BRIDES FOR SIX GIDEONS

HOLIDAYS IN MOUNTAIN HOME

And **collaborative works** ~
on her website ~or~ Amazon's Kristin Holt Page

About the Author

Hi! I'm Kristin Holt, *USA Today* bestselling author of Sweet Romances (G- and PG-rated) set in the Victorian American West.

www.KristinHolt.com

While secular in nature, my titles are "Appropriate for All Audiences" and appeal to selective readers and fans of Christian historical romance.

I love to hear from readers! Please drop me a note: email me at *Kristin@KristinHolt.com*.

I write frequent articles (or *view recent posts easily* on my Home Page, *scroll down*) about the **nineteenth century American west—every subject of possible interest to readers**, amateur historians, authors...as all of these tidbits surfaced while researching for my books.

http://bit.ly/2aiinNC
(case sensitive)

Or find me on Facebook. Here's my FB Profile Page:

http://bit.ly/2axfURD
(case sensitive)

And my Facebook Author Fan Page: *Kristin Holt, Sweet Victorian Western Romance*

http://bit.ly/2avSBG3
(case sensitive)

You're invited to join a fantastic Facebook group for authors and readers of Western Historical Romances, **Pioneer Hearts**.
https://www.facebook.com/groups/pioneerhearts/
or, more simply:
http://bit.ly/1ElS5S8
(case sensitive)

As of summer 2016, Pioneer Hears has almost 2500 Readers and 242 Authors. We talk Western Historical Romance, give away prizes, share books we've loved, announce new releases, and connect as friends.

#PioneerHearts

Please stop by www.KristinHolt.com and say hello!

Kristin

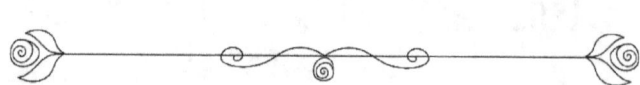